For Andrew, hoping
you enjoy the book.
Eva Abbo

The Crossroads of Yesterday

Eva Abbo

Novel

The Crossroads of Yesterday

I dedicate this book to:

Freddy Abbo, my soul mate, my life companion and the happiness we've shared.

To my beloved:

Ileana, Eran, Larry, Susy, Edward, Jonathan, Michael, Daniella, Daniel, Alexandra, Michael, Ariella, and Gabriel, the lights that illuminate my path.

... and to all my loved ones and dear friends.

Acknowledgments:

To Freddy Abbo for his invaluable computer tutorials, technical assistance and overall support.

To Michael Parker for his professional translation and dedication.

To Carol Montiel for her enthusiasm, precise corrections and interpretation of my thoughts.

To Stefanie Resciniti for the magnificent book cover design.

To Edward Abbo for the contribution of the book cover photo, a beautiful picture of the Abbo's street in Sefat.

Chapter 1

"Congratulations, Mrs. Rotlewicz. You're going to have a baby!

Vivian's eyes widened, as she looked at the doctor and his analytical expression... an oval face... clad in white... who, though no older than she, commanded that air of authority that comes with wide professional knowledge.

"Do you feel ill?" he asked her, concerned, as he saw the color drain from her face.

Hesitating, she took another look at the office surrounding her: the blond wood desk with rounded corners, chairs upholstered in dusty rose-colored material; shelves jammed with books whose worn covers spoke of their use; the doctor's diplomas and certificates carefully placed in black lacquer frames.

"There's no way the test could be wrong?"

"Absolutely not," he immediately replied, in response to his patient's unexpected reaction.

Upset, she averted her gaze toward the window and remained silent for several minutes. Then she stood up. "Thank you doctor. That was all I wanted to know."

"I'll expect you next month for a routine prenatal checkup."

After saying goodbye, she walked rapidly through the medical building's hallways, carpeted in shades of aquamarine, and took the elevator to the basement of the building where her burgundy-colored Mercedes-Benz was parked. As soon as she had started the motor, she punched the accelerator, anxious to get away from the clinic as soon as possible.

The luxurious automobile made its way down busy city streets until it reached a confined private beach surrounded by lush greenery and set off by some tall, wild grapevines.

As soon as she got out of the car, she removed her high-heeled shoes and began to walk along a narrow, twisting pine boardwalk. Her slim, attractive figure slid lightly between the railings; her strong, well-formed legs took on speed, at times, to the rhythm of her accelerated heartbeat. A strong wind tangled her long, lustrous blond hair, perfectly styled minutes before. Two heavy tears flooded the green of her luminous eyes and prevented her making out the path; then they slipped down her delicate, anguished face, further deepening her desire to flee, to hide. She closed her full, red lips tightly and ran…ran till she reached the golden sand where she let herself fall to the ground as she covered her twisted face with her hands, breaking into strong cries until these became deep sobs. She wept, letting go of tremendous pain that consumed her and finally, now weary, she sighed with resignation.

"Dear God, what will happen to my baby" she thought, profoundly upset. "Doesn't it have a right to live just like any other human being? How can I interrupt its development if it's already started to grow?"

"No, not in a million years!" she shouted, her mind made up. She wouldn't let it be destroyed. "It's my baby! I'll fight anyone on this—myself included, if I have to—for it to be born and to be happy. Now I'm glad about the decision I made, when I began to think I was pregnant—to see a doctor, chosen at random—to make sure. He doesn't know what my real problem is, and that gives me time, a chance to think calmly about my actions and their possible future consequences."

Day became night. The heavens were shining serenely, cloudless, the background to spectacular stars whose silvery brilliance began to be seen across the vastness of the firmament.

Suddenly she was cold. A slight shiver coursed through her.

She clutched her olive-green linen jacket to her body, adjusted the silken scarf knotted about her neck and got up, now feeling calmer.

It's time to get home, she thought. Victor must be wondering where I am.

Chapter 2

The light changed. Seeing it turn green, Vivian let off the brake, accelerated, and turned to the right, guiding her vehicle along a highway bordered by a lake on both sides, from which sprung two extraordinary fountains, their waters in constant movement. She soon crossed a whitewashed concrete bridge before reaching the security gate.

She inserted her key card into the slot, and the wooden gate immediately rose to give access to the Boca West residential compound.

Advancing along a wide avenue, she made out the silhouette of two modern structures, the social and golf clubs, lit by streetlights placed at regular intervals along the avenue. She steered left toward the Oakbrook subdivision, where she lived.

It had been twenty-five years since her in-laws had decided to move from Connecticut to Boca Raton, Florida, tired of harsh, months-long winters, in search of weather better suited to their age, with the idea that they could enjoy their favorite pastime—golf—year round.

Given their excellent financial status, a condition enjoyed as a result of Abraham Rotlewicz's intense years of work in his jewelry store, they had acquired a sumptuous mansion with enormous picture windows featuring views of the canal, not far from the famous Boca Raton Hotel.

Her young husband's childhood and adolescence had unfolded in that opulent setting surrounded by luxuries. Later he went to medical school at Harvard, where his enormous potential and interests earned him both prestige and distinction.

Once he had set up his practice, in a modern, centrally located downtown building, and with a number of patients to his credit, he decided to spend a bit of his time enjoying himself. One night, coming out of Pete's Restaurant, a mutual friend introduced him to Vivian, and from that moment on they were inseparable.

At the end of eight months, Victor proposed marriage. Thrilled, she accepted with a passionate kiss.

The engagement, the wedding and the honeymoon passed in a flurry of glasses filled with Dom Perignon, orchids, extravagant wedding gifts, happiness and congratulations. Everything turned out just as imagined, and all four in-laws, elated, made the event their favorite topic of conversation, exchanging photos and sharing even the smallest details with relatives, friends and anyone who would listen.

After intensely enjoyable stays in a number of European nations, they established themselves in the magnificent residence of solid red brick, beveled glass windows and imported roof tiles that had been a wedding gift from both their parents. The property was placed in an exclusive area whose every element had been minutely studied and planned out by famous architects; the result was a relaxed, idyllic environ made up of residential subdivisions among which Oakbrook stood out for its beauty, luxury and originality.

Expansive golf courses and vast lakes could be seen all around and a great variety of trees and other luxuriant landscaping, strategically planted, lent the development a singularly aesthetic touch.

Some days following their return to Boca Raton, Victor went back to work, at which time Alex Vorlowesky was able to take some very well-earned time off; in Victor's absence, his partner had taken on running the entire practice.

Vivian felt happy. She was deeply in love with her husband who, besides his innate air of distinction was tall, and young—twenty-nine—with dark chestnut hair, was attractive...and had a special way of treating her that made him irreplaceable.

Delighted, she would often wander about her surroundings: the large foyer, decorated daily with exotic flower arrangements in a plethora of colors, placed in clear glass vases supported by greenish, brown and gray iron-work, fashioned into unparalleled and original designs. An enormous chandelier of fine Czechoslovakian crystal asserted itself majestically, serenely balanced above this space designed exclusively for her. A wide bank of gray marble stairs, their edges rounded, ascended dramatically to a landing dominated by a large antique painting, and then split at the second story along separate staircases to the left and the right.

The living room was furnished with two earth-toned sofas in combination with aristocratic armchairs upholstered in tiger-skin, featuring numerous cushions and throw pillows in caramel and terra cotta shades, placed at random. A wooden coffee table and occasional tables, artistically carved, topped with crystal and silver adornments; original paintings by Dalí, masterfully chosen by an art expert; and the magnificent black Steinway grand piano, the faithful witness to its owner's hours of practice and hard work.

There was a classic Chippendale dining room whose furniture was upholstered in aquamarine fabric and in a variety of contrasts and motifs, complemented by a carved, dark wood sideboard whose beveled glass vitrine housed splendid Rosenthal china, a gift from her maternal grandmother and a possession of inestimable value and pride to Vivian.

Travertine floors extended everywhere throughout the first floor until reaching the large, immaculate kitchen, in light wood paneling, outfitted with the latest high-tech appliances.

The garage's automatic door rose slowly to make way for the car waiting outside, and Vivian skillfully parked it beside the navy blue Maserati that belonged to her husband.

She stepped down from the car gracefully and as soon as she was inside the house, Chivas—the shiny, golden Retriever, wagging her tail with excitement and doting affection—rushed up to receive and welcome her.

Vivian made out a light from beneath the study door and letting go of the loyal pet she caressed, ran up the stairs toward her bedroom.

"I should shower and change clothes," she thought. "Victor shouldn't see me this way. I haven't decided when to tell him I'm pregnant."

Chapter 3

Vivian observed her face at length, in the long, wide mirror of the master bedroom's boudoir; to make sure any trace of tears had disappeared. She smoothed out the skirt of her blue linen dress with the palm of her hand and made her way to the stairs.

She hesitated a moment before opening the study door, but thought better of it when she saw what time it was. She entered and immediately felt a hot gust from the fireplace surround her entire body. She looked toward the wide, dark, carved-wood desk that supported a fresh spray of oversized fern leaves, like so much lace, and an oval-shaped silver frame that held an evocative wedding photo, in which two rings were exchanged along with a promise of eternal love. She directed her attention to a wide, gray leather armchair—but her husband was not there. She continued to scan, more intensely, and soon she spied a figure by the windowsill, in deep concentration, looking towards the world outside.

"Victor," she called to him with tenderness.

"Darling, you're finally here. I was worried about you!" her husband exclaimed, turning to look at her.

"I'm sorry I didn't call—the day flew by and I just lost track."

"No worries," he replied, drawing near so as to take her in his arms.

"How I longed for you to be near in all those difficult moments," she thought as he hugged her, then reacted by returning his embrace strongly, as if life depended on it.

"Did something happen, honey? I can tell there's something on your mind."

She broke from him slightly and looked into his eyes, and for a split second was ready to tell the truth.

Suddenly the telephone rang and, without thinking much about it, he extended his arm to pick it up. As he spoke, Vivian watched him in silence, barely able to concentrate on what he was saying. After a few minutes the conversation ended abruptly and Victor spoke somewhat gravely of an emergency.

"I'm sorry, Vivian, but I've got to go right away. There's an emergency at the hospital. One of my patients has gone into labor and they need me there. I'll come home just as soon as I can," he said as he snatched his lab coat from an oaken coat hook. "I love you," he added, kissing her on the mouth and hurrying out, shutting the door.

Vivian was struck by her husband's sudden departure. By now she ought to be used to it—being the wife of a gynecologist and obstetrician required patience—but the void his absences left in their wake always hit her hard. She slowly went to the sofa that sat before the fireplace, stoked the fire with a long bronze poker, and then collapsed on the elegant, comfortable seat.

Smoke, heat and sparks rose from the expansive flames, suffusing the atmosphere with an unending dance of shifting shapes and widths, all followed in absorbed contemplation through Vivian's warm, exotic green eyes. Her mind meandered past meaningless precincts when suddenly she stopped short before a significant past memory. Her body tensed, she closed her fists, grew pale, and suffered from a painful grimace that traced itself across her face.

She remembered with ghastly precision that summer afternoon, five years ago, when she had been in the kitchen, decorating a birthday cake for Victor. Then her heart was filled with intense excitement, in anticipation of the surprise party she was putting on that very night, an occasion for some one hundred guests. Skillfully she spread the fine, sugary frosting she'd made earlier, across the cake, just like she'd learned in her pastry-making class. When she was satisfied with the results, she added other decorative touches.

"Oh, Miss Vivian, how beautiful the cake looks!" exclaimed Vicky, one of the housekeepers.

"Thank you," Vivian replied, pleased, as she picked up the cake stand and prepared to carry it into the dining room. She pushed open the kitchen door with her back, and just as she crossed the doorframe she felt a penetrating pain at a point in her head, plus a jarring chill that ran the length of her body. She brought her arms in to prevent her precious cargo from falling, but in vain; her muscles gave way as the enormous burden fell to the floor with a thunderous racket, smashing into countless pieces, followed by an inert being that slid down beside it.

"Maria! Carmen! Miss Vivian has fainted; please, help me get her up!" shouted Vicky, overwhelmed.

Uniting their strength, they managed to pick her up and take her to the living room settee.

"Wake up, Miss Vivian," pleaded Maria, beside herself. "Please, answer me—it upsets us to see you this way."

"Please don't scare us, Miss Vivian," added Carmen, sobbing as she saw her mistress's kind face grow pale.

"She's not responding—we'd better get the doctor on the phone. He'll know how to handle this," Vicky volunteered nervously.

Victor was listening to a patient's chest when his nurse rushed into his examining room.

"What's happening, Yolanda—why all the excitement?" he asked, disarmed.

"Your wife has fainted and the household staff is hysterical. I called the paramedics and they're on their way to your house."

Victor looked at her, horrified, and dashed from the office in seconds.

"Vivian, darling, I'm here by your side...please, please say something and tell me you're all right," he besought her, between sobs, as he walked next to the stretcher they were using to convey her body to the ambulance.

The deafening noise of the siren echoed as the ambulance demanded passage among the regular Glades Road traffic. It went forward some distance, crossed to the right, reaching Thirteenth Street, where it veered to the left and took a sharp turn until arriving at Boca Raton Hospital.

"My wife is young, 23 years old, and she's never been sick. What could have happened?" Victor wondered, painfully, pacing back and forth across the comfortable, if brightly lit waiting room, wishing he'd spot the doctor coming out from surgery.

Time passed with infuriating calm, especially in light of the tortuous uncertainty of the moment, when suddenly Dr. Gerard Cohen came up to him.

"Doctor, how is she?"

"She's conscious, and in general her condition has improved; that terrible pallor in her face has disappeared. I administered an I.V. muscle relaxant and she's calm now, resting."

"But why did she pass out?" Victor asked anxiously.

"Right now it's too soon to establish a definite diagnosis. We did a number of basic tests to rule out the possibility of any serious cerebral function damage, but to double-check, we need to do some more specific testing."

From that point forward, under strict medical supervision, Vivian underwent infinite tests and diagnostic studies. A number were painful and drawn out. She was in the hospital for one week, leading to a state of terrible depression that she had never previously known.

One day Victor reached the bed where Vivian lay. With a surprise kiss, he excitedly told her:

"Darling, we finally finished the tests and you can come home with me today. This hospital stay and all the invasive exams that have happened here will soon seem like just some nightmare you once had."

Just then the kindly figure of Dr. Cohen came in, wearing his traditional lab coat. They watched his unsteady gait as he entered.

Vivian carefully observed his sallow, nervous face, topped with scant gray hairs, and she was seized with a terrible upset. Maybe it was a premonition that came over her as she confirmed her affliction in his intelligent, amber-colored eyes.

"Mrs. Rotlewicz, Dr. Rotlewicz, I hoped to have good news for you, but after undertaking a thorough study of the case, and looking at the outcomes, I'm sorry to say we've discovered what we call a congenital arteriovenous malformation."

Victor blinked several times, seeking to disguise the spectral fear born in that moment of anguish, fear that coursed through his entire being. But his wife's puzzled expression was reflected in the transparency of his pupils, eliminating all doubt.

"I'm in bad shape," she said incredulously, more as an affirmation than a question. She felt her aching heart race.

The doctor's nodded assent confirmed her suspicions.

"What chance do I have for recovery?" she worriedly asked.

"I don't know," Dr. Cohen answered frankly. "In recent decades medicine has advanced exceptionally in certain specialties, but when it comes to congenital malformations we're still just making baby steps."

"So, what comes next?" Victor wondered, trying not to show the terrible pain that had lodged in his heart.

"For the time being, I am planning on prescribing an anti-convulsive to prevent another episode like the one we saw this time. My advice is to take it easy and try to rest as much as possible...and under no circumstances—I have to insist on this, no exceptions—are you to get pregnant."

Vivian's face grew ashen and her eyes opened widely.

"God, no! Never have a baby? Never?" she screamed in torment as she felt two heavy tears run down her face.

Victor ran over and enveloped her in his forceful arms. He started to open his mouth, to say something consoling, but it was then that a hard knot seized his breast, forcing him to choke back horrifying groans.

The return home that day was shrouded in a wave of melancholy, despite the perennial company and repeated efforts on the part of family and friends to make them forget the terrible augur that had been burned into their brains. Painful weeks passed, then visits became less frequent. Indifference took root in Vivian's existence, in contrast to Victor's incessant desperation to save her life.

"You can't understand, Alex," Victor would tell him, upset and holding his head in his hands. "My life has no meaning without her. I love her with all my soul—like I've never loved anyone else. I studied so hard for so many years to become a doctor, I've done a good job at it; I work day and night for the good of my patients...but when it comes to my wife I feel frustrated and powerless to do anything for her."

Alex broke his friend and partner's gaze sheepishly, unable to witness the crushing pain that was torturing him. He looked around where they were sitting. It was an elegant, ample bar and restaurant conveniently located nearby the practice, done in the style of the 1930s. There were heavy velvet curtains in scarlet, long mirrors partially covering the walls, and gilt sconces adjusted to cast a cozy, indirect light, alongside imposing period artworks. The proprietor inherited the antique furnishings in leather and sculpted wood. Somewhat dazzled, Alex contemplated the magnificent reflection in the glass. The varied colors came from countless bottles resting on precisely mounted and aligned shelves, along various wall panels. This created a sense of depth proper to the bar.

"Will you have another whisky, doctor?" asked the bartender.

Awakened from a deep momentary distraction, he adjusted his body on the high bench and assented to the question, then refocused on his troubled companion.

"I cant lose her—I just can't!" he repeated, frustrated, slamming his fist once and again against the high, olive-colored marble bar.

"Hey, take it easy," Alex practically begged, exasperated. "It won't happen! I promise. If there's anything in the world that can possibly help her, no matter how crazy, we'll find it. You can be certain of that."

Chapter 4

Summer heat softened to make way for autumn's unequaled, iridescent rays. Leaves slipped to the ground slowly, denuding trunks and branches whose trembling blanket in shades of green, orange, and yellow transformed into withered, dusty husks. Following nature's cycle, a raw snowfall irreverently descended, covering the earth's contours like a white canvas, penetrating to its most recondite depths, chilling Northern neighbors and, in some cases, as finances allowed, moved them to flee to warmer climes.

The arrival of so many people to Florida's various cities led to crowds in the state's places of public accommodation—as well as exhaustive, inexhaustible activity throughout the Boca Raton Hospital—allowing Victor's mind to stray at times from the inevitable sentence that hung over Vivian's life.

Days went by, tedious and unchanging for Vivian, voluntarily shut into the master bedroom. Such few times as she moved about her house she did so as would an automaton, and was a source of deep pain to her husband and family as they remembered the innate cheer that once characterized her and with which she had once infused anything around her. Yet once she knew she could not be a mother—motherhood being her most fervent desire—nothing in life had any meaning.

One winter morning at the beginning of the New Year, Victor, dressed in his habitual starched white lab coat, was listening carefully to the chest of a patient in her eighth month of pregnancy. At the same time, Alex was waiting impatiently in the adjoining examination room, pacing to stifle an impulse to interrupt his partner's work.

"You can get dressed now, Mrs. Smith. I find both you and your child in perfect health," he declared, slipping the stethoscope from around his neck and gently resting it on a small gray Formica worktable next to the examination bench. "Keep up the same diet, take the calcium and the vitamins that I prescribed. I'll see you again in fifteen days."

"Thank you, doctor."

Victor traced out a vague smile for his patient as he said goodbye, then focused on her clinical history in order to add the needed note.

"Oh, ma'am, I'm so sorry!" Alex exclaimed with embarrassment, nearly tripping over the patient in his haste to enter the exam room. "I hope I didn't hurt you."

"No worries, doctor. I'm fine," she replied as she walked away.

"Victor: get up—let's get out of here."

Three deep delineated wrinkles formed in his forehead, as he looked up to see his partner who so urgently called him.

"What is it, Alex?" he asked with curiosity.

"Right this minute, here in this hospital, a Canadian doctor—thought to be preeminent in his specialty—is giving a talk on congenital malformations."

"Let's go!" Victor shouted, elated, jumping up from his blue swivel chair, dropping a flurry of papers as he stepped away.

The short stretch of spotless white hospital hallway, suffused with the acrid, penetrating stench of disinfectant, became an eternity for the long-suffering husband. When they reached the lecture hall, he forcibly pushed open its heavy, lacquered wood double doors, acquiring a full view of the crowded chamber. Victor continued walking in, always closely followed by the figure of his friend, moving down the clay-colored stair-carpet. He picked out two seats in the second row, upholstered in a thick, cream-colored corduroy, which they managed to reach—though not without some difficulty, since their progress required jostling a number of onlookers.

An enormous light flooded the auditorium floor thanks to thousands of rays whose sparkle refracted through wide windows to create a fairyland of suspended particles and intertwined rainbows.

Dr. Samuel Guberek's precise diction resounded vigorously and correctly, boosted by a powerful microphone, as he explained the details of his most recent research and operations.

Focused on the speaker's athletic figure, Victor hung on his every word. Suddenly an intense shiver coursed through his form.

"My God!" he exclaimed, excited. "He's referring to Vivian's disease." Alex turned his head to where he spotted his colleague and saw him grow pale.

"Outcomes acquired by means of this intervention have been successful in some eighty-five percent of cases," the physician pronounced. "However, the patient's physical and psychological condition must be studied in depth and necessary precautions must be taken before proceeding to eliminate the origin of the congenital malformations."

Victor's heart raced as the lecture moved on to other subjects. A thousand thoughts converged in his head and kept him from focusing.

"God, I hope he finishes soon," he quipped to Alex under his breath. "I've got to talk to him right away." Another half-hour of uncertainty passed and as soon as Victor saw him conclude his presentation and look down to gather his notes, spread across a thick, rectangular glass table, he quickly went over to him.

"Dr. Guberek, my name is Victor Rotlewicz, I'm a gynecologist and obstetrician here at the hospital and I need to speak to you about my wife's critical condition. I'm hoping you can help me."

The specialist was tall, tanned, with dark black eyes, brown hair, a moustache and an athletic frame; his age was undetermined. He left aside the task of packing his things into a fine, black leather attaché resting on one of several chairs made of a mustard-colored wood. He then focused his attention on the young physician who stared back at him with infinite, if contained, anxiety.

"It's nice to meet you, Dr. Rotlewicz. How can I help?"

"My wife, Vivian, has been diagnosed with an incurable arteriovenous congenital malformation. She doesn't have much time left according to her doctor," added Victor, his speech labored, peering at Dr. Guberek through eyes clouded by two thick tears set to fall at any moment. "Please, doctor—you've got to help her!" Taking pity on this unfortunate man and the wife he loved, he put his right hand on Victor Rotlewicz's shoulder as he spoke:

"I'll do everything I can to work with the two of you. Bring her to Dr. Hector Greenberg's office at 3:30. She needs to be examined as soon as possible."

Vivian finished buttoning her white silk blouse, trimmed in lace, and smoothed out her navy blue skirt with her hand, as was her habit. Then she put a wide, woven belt around her slim waistline; slipped her elegant, caramel-colored Italian-leather shoes onto her diminutive feet and grabbed her handbag as she fastened it. She briskly left the cubicle where she had been and headed to office 215, where her husband and Dr. Guberek awaited her.

"Please take a seat, Mrs. Rotlewicz," the physician requested, standing and pulling out the chair with a courteous gesture.

"As I was explaining to Victor just a few minutes before you got here, I think it is advisable to operate in your case, but—," he added imperiously, "you both must completely understand the serious risks to which you will be exposed..."

A jubilant twinkle shone from Vivian's emerald-green eyes and she calmly agreed with a broad nod.

"Go on, doctor! There's nothing to lose, and without the operation my life is hanging from a thread."

"In that case," responded Dr. Guberek, "you'll need to transfer without delay to the hospital in Montreal where I work. Here's my card, with my address and my phone number so you can make an appointment with my secretary. In the meantime I will contact her to simplify the procedure and so we can get underway as soon as possible."

After many preparations for the trip and an intensive operation in the Montreal's hospital, Victor crept quietly up to the foot of the spotless bed in the intensive care unit where his wife had lain for some hours, recovering from the delicate operation she had undergone. His heart shuddered to see her exhausted body there, connected via innumerable tubes and wires to a number of machines, each plugged into its own monitor. Her head was wrapped in a turban made of thick, off white bandages. Her face was hollow and expressionless; her lids heavy over half-opened eyes. An endotracheal tube came out of her mouth and plugged into a respirator at the same time the dried outer corner of her lips let loose a thick trail of saliva.

Not wishing to spend more time contemplating her pitiful state, he turned his gaze leftward to a closed window, and seconds later imagined—almost like a visualization in his mind—Vivian's slim figure as it made its way around the house by means of graceful and rhythmical movements. He perceived the penetrating, rarefied jasmine aroma of her perfume; stroked her long, silky golden hair, saw her porcelain-like face, admired the contours of her refined nose and the thickness of her seductive lips.

"Oh, God!" he exclaimed between sobs, upset and covering his face.

"Victor..." he heard a voice, like a whisper.

"Sweetheart," he immediately responded, drying his tears and running to her side.

She moved her head on the pillow and squeezing her hand against his, attempted a smile—maybe more like a grimace—and closed her eyes.

"Vivian, Vivian," he called out in anguish.

Unanswered, he got up and went off in search of the practitioner on duty.

"What seems to be the problem?" asked an obese nurse.

"My wife woke up, said my name, squeezed my hand and went back under."

When she got to the room, the corpulent figure studied the patient carefully and after verifying normal levels as reflected on the monitor, testing the patient's reflexes, the reaction to light in her pupils, and blood oxygen saturation, she spoke more calmly.

"I'm not surprised by what's happened; we gave her a muscle relaxant to keep her resting calmly, avoid upsets and too much coughing that wouldn't be good for her brain right now. In the meantime, the respirator connected to the trachea through her mouth is doing the breathing for her."

"I've come for Mrs. Rotlewicz," said a young black man. Tall and slim with curly hair, prominent eyes and thick lips, the orderly went over to her bed pushing a prepared stretcher without a pillow. "The doctor requested a digital scan."

"Get some rest, doctor," the kind nurse suggested, noting the extreme exhaustion his face reflected. "It's been a hard day for you," she added with certainty.

Vivian's recuperation started off as a slow, difficult process that required large doses of willpower, patience and understanding. Her hospital and convalescent stay extended over two months, which meant Victor often traveled to Canada in an attempt to divide his time and attention between his wife and his patients back in Boca Raton.

Lea Rotlewicz had reached the third floor of the hospital in Canada. She made her way down the wide hallway resolutely, precisely following the instructions that the receptionist had just given her. At the same time her heart raced at the thought of being reunited with her daughter-in-law Vivian, and in just a few moments.

A noble bearing, graceful gestures and a refined taste in clothes were the hallmarks of that extraordinary and resigned woman. Gray-haired with a calm brow, prominent cheekbones and a square-face, there was a sparkle in her blue eyes. Her slim figure lent her a youthful-looking appearance despite her fifty-four years.

She knocked twice and on the third attempt heard a voice intone, "Come in."

She went in nervously and when she saw Vivian seated there on a brown-leather armchair, dressed in a silky, aquamarine robe, she hastened over to embrace her, at the same time an incessant flow of tears fell across her daughter-in-law's porcelain-complexion face.

"As soon as Victor came back to Boca Raton," she said, moved, "I made the decision to come see you. I imagined you were lonely and I wanted to keep you company. Your parents haven't been able to travel because of the financial difficulties they're going through right now."

A wave of gratitude swept over Vivian from the deepest part of her being and despite being unable to find the words to describe so sublime a sentiment, she embraced Lea tightly, sobbing, hoping to transmit the way she felt.

"Don't cry, my dear, you've just been through something really painful" she said sadly, taking note of the swollen and red incision that extended from the upper edge of her forehead to the rear of her cranium. "The future will repay you, with interest, for the agony you've been through. You won't ever have to fear for your life again when it comes to this disease—it's been removed at the source. Your husband—who adores you—will continue to provide you with love and happiness."

"But," Vivian added, upset, "there's an important, decisive factor that comes into having that future you mention."

An expression of doubt framed Lea Rotlewicz's benevolent face and she blinked quickly and nervously when she heard Vivian declare:

"I want to have a baby! No matter what it costs me!"

In his private office at the end of a month, Dr. Samuel Guberek issued his post-op diagnosis in the presence of Vivian, Victor and his mother.

"I'm quite satisfied with the operation's outcomes and the patient's excellent recovery. That said," he added, taking care with his words, "we should take certain permanent precautions to avoid any possible relapse."

"What do you mean, doctor?" asked Victor, with a trace of anxiety.

"I've prescribed an anti-convulsive for Vivian that she should take as prescribed for the rest of her life to avoid any unpleasant surprises. But its side effects mean that pregnancy is absolutely contraindicated."

"NO! It just can't be!" shouted Vivian, hysterical.

Chapter 5

The Rotlewicz family's return home was wrapped in a thick cloud of melancholy. The idea of never ever hearing a little one's footfall on the marble floors, of never hearing the echo of a child's laughter there, or not being able to see an innocent glance in a child's tender eyes, curious before the unknown, was intolerable to them. Vivian decided to smother her pain amid unending hours at the piano and working as an interior decorator, at the same time Victor sought to comfort her, and tried to resign himself to his fate, spending long hours at the office.

Five trying, painful years passed in this way, when suddenly there was a miracle: she was pregnant.

Some strange sound from the glimmering, sparking flames that danced incessantly over logs in the fireplace recaptured Vivian's attention and shook her out of her reverie, obliging her to face the reality of the present.

"I won't say anything about it to anyone until the baby starts to grow," she exclaimed aloud, getting up from the sofa in a series of rapid movements. "Otherwise they'll try to get me to have an abortion. And I won't—ever—even if it means risking my life." A rare, disturbing glint lit out from her green eyes, echoing her heart's rapid palpitations.

I should cut down on the anti-convulsive the doctor gave me, until I can quit it for good, she thought, unsettled, as she paced the room, especially now, during the baby's fetal phase. I hope my body reacts okay to not taking it—otherwise the consequences could be awful.

Time passed, along with six months of waiting as Vivian's anguished expectations intensified and she watched the changes that were transforming her body.

"Dear God," she fervently pleaded, "please don't let anything happen to me. Let me carry this child to term."

One spring morning, Vivian was bent over her garden, tending some flowers, when her mother-in-law approached her.

"The rose garden looks gorgeous," she declared, impressed, taking in the details of her surroundings.

"I've given it a lot of work—and it's taken a lot of patience," Vivian responded with pleasure, as she placed a metal trowel atop a henequen sack of peat moss. When she stood, she held onto the brim of her hat, defending herself from a gust of wind.

"I want to speak just us—alone."

A presentiment—and an accurate one at that—caused Vivian to shudder. "You know my secret," she exclaimed in fear.

"Yes, I do," Lea answered with a pained expression.

"At first as I watched you gain weight, I had my doubts, since I know how responsible you are. I know you're aware of the doctor's warning to avoid pregnancy at all costs because of the anticonvulsive horrible side effects. But now I'm sure! How can you risk your life and that of an innocent child who's growing inside you?"

Upset, Vivian looked away from the accusatory face and focused on a leafy tree, her favorite, with its thick, magnificent trunk, long, gnarled and assertive branches, and its infinite, abundant leaves floating in the open air.

"I'm not hurting my baby," she said with conviction. "I've stopped taking the medicine."

"You must be joking!" Lea responded, alarmed.

"I tapered off gradually and carefully watched how my body reacted, until I stopped taking it completely."

"Did you consult Victor about this?"

Vivian shook her head no, repeatedly.

"But, sweetheart, why?"

"He would have pushed me to have an abortion, to avoid risking my life, and would have suggested adopting again."

"Please, you've got to tell him," Lea begged, alarmed, "He's the father of that child and he has a right to know. As a doctor he can evaluate the situation professionally and help you get through the last months of the pregnancy."

"You can't be serious...!" Victor shouted, incredulously, as he grasped his head firmly between his hands.

"I'm sorry I couldn't tell you sooner but I was afraid of how you'd react," Vivian whispered between her teeth, growing pale.

"You don't get how serious this is," he snapped angrily. "I'm going to ask for a consultation in Montreal right away with Dr. Guberek. He's a specialist and he'll know what we need to do next."

Victor hung up the telephone and sat frozen at a carved wood and granite console, thinking about the conversation he'd just had with his colleague, before walking back toward the living room where Vivian and his mother were assuredly waiting.

There's nothing else to do, he thought desperately, but keep the faith, pray, and wait patiently to see how things turn out...

Chapter 6

"It's a beautiful baby girl!" the obstetrician exclaimed, thrilled. In spite of having attended countless deliveries, he still felt an intense emotion when he caught this particular newborn, so tender, naïve and tiny, a breath of life and innocence.

Vivian breathed a sigh of relief when she heard the little girl's vigorous, infantile cries, now unmolested by the tremendous burden that during interminable months had weighed on her heart. At the same time Victor took her hand, his eyes flooded with an overwhelming torrent of tears, and he raised a heartfelt prayer of thanks to the Almighty, knowing that his wife and daughter were out of all danger.

Starting then, a feeling of joy washed over the existence of every family member. Abraham and Lea put on a gala entertainment at home, widely attended, to celebrate their beloved granddaughter's official naming as Evelyn Rotlewicz, in honor of a distinguished, unforgettable great-grandmother on her father's side.

"Alone at last after so much hullaballoo!" Victor exclaimed, drawing near to his wife and enveloping her in his vigorous arms.

"It was an enchanting night," she whispered into his ear.

"Not more enchanting than my two little ladies," he added jokingly, and kissed her passionately on the mouth.

"Let's go see her in her room," Vivian suggested, as soon as she caught her breath, leading her husband by the hand, scurrying excitedly up the stairs to reach the second floor landing.

The nurse greeted them as they went by, picking up in their glances the intense love, tenderness and pride that the angelical little being, then asleep, elicited in them.

"I wish she were awake," said Victor, disappointed.

"She's a perfect little child," declared the nurse with a professional air.

Five wonderful years of life passed, like a dream.

Evelyn, attired in a gauzy dress of white organdy, standing tall in her shiny, black patent leather shoes, blew out the twinkling candles that had been carefully placed on an enormous cake decorated with a wide variety of roses confected of aquamarine-colored frosting. Evelyn's favorite color stood out most of all.

"Yea!"—Nearly a hundred excited children called out, clapping their hands.

Beside himself with joy, Victor missed nothing as he

hid one eye behind a late-model video camera, shifting from here to there, intermittently attracting the attention of his beloved daughter. The innocent, pink-faced little girl was crowned in curls the color of the setting sun, and blessed with two extraordinary blue jewels, unusually transparent, for eyes. Her agile, proportioned form moved with unparalleled grace.

Vivian hugged her tightly, wishing her a world of joy, health and blessings.

Evelyn extricated herself from the embrace and affectionately kissing her mother's smooth cheek, took her best friend Natalie's hand and casually ran off toward where her playmates were.

With a mother's pride, Vivian followed her daughter's activities in a tender glance, when suddenly for two or three seconds she remembered the fear and anxiety she had lived during the pregnancy. Her body tensed at the thought of someday losing her.

"What's wrong, darling?" Victor asked as he drew near, worried from the moment he saw her reaction through his viewfinder.

"It's nothing. I was just remembering the past and got scared. Forget about it."

"Daddy, mommy! Come here! I'm going to open my presents!" they heard Evelyn say excitedly.

"Then let's go," responded Victor right away.

Day became night and after making sure that their daughter was sleeping, Vivian carefully closed the door to her bedroom for fear of waking her up and made her way to the master bedroom, where she undressed. She buttoned her lilac, silk and lace nightgown, put on some matching slippers and sat on the scarlet bench in front of her custom-made, wrought iron vanity and began, as always, the delicate feminine gestures that constituted brushing her thick, lustrous hair.

From the bed, Victor watched her in the mirror, dazzled by his wife's slender figure. He could not wait any longer and called her to his side.

She got up, pleased, abandoning her hairbrush on the bureau, turned out the light and slipped between the silken sheets to return her beloved's embrace.

The two bodies moved about the bed's circumscribed space, kissing and caressing, sensing that an enormous wave of passion enveloped them, when suddenly a horrifying scream echoed throughout the house.

"What is *that*?" Vivian asked, shaken and lifting her head.

"I don't know," he responded hoarsely, frozen in place.

"It's Evelyn!" she shouted as she sprang to her feet.

Upset, they both burst into their daughter's bedroom, and from the doorway they saw her body twist in violent, uncontrolled movements as her contorted face reflected intense pain.

"Don't take him from me, please...NO!" she shouted between sobs, terrified, with her eyes closed.

"Calm down, sweetheart," Vivian begged, drawing closer. "Daddy and I are here with you."

"Don't leave me, Duvid! I can't live without you!" the little girl continued to beg, shaken, as her parents exchanged a quick glace filed with uncertainty.

"Evelyn, wake up," shouted Victor, authoritatively, as she rose up from the bed.

"Where am I? What happened?" she asked, confused, opening her eyes.

"You've had a terrible nightmare," Vivian answered. She hugged her daughter. "But it's all over now. Lie down and go back to sleep."

"Good night, princess," Victor murmured, wrapping himself around her and brushing his lips against the little girl's delicate cheek.

"Good night," she answered drowsily.

"This has been a pretty hectic day for her," added Vivian as she shut the bedroom door.

The enigmatic dream came back to Evelyn on a number of occasions, at random intervals, to the anguished frustration of her confused parents, who could not understand the inchoate meaning of their little girl's inscrutable words.

One morning, Vivian received a call from the Boca Raton Academy principal and—picking up on the rapid way the esteemed woman was expressing herself—abandoned her work, dressed rapidly and headed out to meet her.

"Please have a seat, Mrs. Rotlewicz," the educator exhorted as soon as Vivian entered her office. "Would you like a cup of tea?"

"I'd be delighted," she responded, adding a tender smile to her words.

As Mrs. Sudarsky requested the secretary bring in

the refreshments, Vivian took advantage of the time to closely inspect the heavy, carved, dark-wood antique furniture; the matching shelves loaded with books of varying titles and styles; and paintings framed in gilt, renaissance style, all evincing the most refined taste. No doubt the faithful reflection of their owner, who that afternoon wore a grey silken dress by Anne Klein, set off by a thick, matte gold chain and matching earrings. She wore her salt-and-pepper hair in a sleek bun, Grace Kelly-style, and it served as the frame for the school principal's plump, good-natured face.

"Above all, Mrs. Rotlewicz," she said as she sat down in a comfortable olive-green suede armchair positioned behind her desk, "I want you to know how much I appreciate your having come to see me right away. As soon as you understand why there was such a rush, I think you'll grant I was right."

Vivian nodded in agreement, allowing the school principal to go on.

"Since about three months ago, both Evelyn's professors and I have noted a rather marked change in her behavior. At first we decided to watch her closely, in case it was just something having to do with her age of if we were worrying in vain, but over the days, this change has grown increasingly obvious. Softness and sweetness, innate to her personality, have been disappearing in favor of a child who is misbehaved, disobedient and fussy."

Vivian's body shuddered involuntarily as she took in the principal's words; her face tightened and blanched and her eyes widened wildly in a reflection of consternation and fear.

"Her classmates avoid her because she treats them bad," Mrs. Sudarsky went on. "Even Natalie, who until now was her best friend, shuns her. Her marks have declined visibly and her behavior has become intolerable. I would like to know if you, your husband or some other close relative has noted any apparent changes in her behavior at home."

"She's having nightmares," whispered Vivian.

"Only on occasion or repeatedly?" principal Sudarsky asked. "Have you been able to decipher any meanings?"

"At first they were more intermittent, but in the last month or so they have repeated more frequently and have grown more intense. While the dream lasts, Evelyn changes, suffering strong, violent shocks that alternate with pain, begging, and tears. She asks for mercy for someone named Duvid and begs not to be taken away from him. We've also heard two other names: Ariel and Ethel.

"Mrs. Rotlewicz, do you recognize any of those names?"

"To be honest, no," she answered anxiously. "We managed to figure out the origin of the name Duvid, through help from my mother-in-law, who speaks fluent Yiddish; it's the equivalent to David. But it's strange to hear that coming from Evelyn's mouth, since she doesn't know the language...she's had no exposure to it at any time in her life. As for Ariel, we do know some people, now older, in the community who are named Ariel, though I seriously doubt that Evelyn has had any contact with any of them. The name Ethel does strike me as strange—I've never known anyone with that name. I have a friend named Etty, but that's hardly the same."

After their conversation—and with the girl's parent's permission—the school principal assigned Evelyn's case to Dr. Peggy Colton, the school psychologist, a *suma cum laude* Harvard graduate.

Chapter 7

"*Azoi vil ich mehr nisht leben. Main veilt, un zei, iz gurnisch wert. Gott meine, schreck zei oder struf zei nish mit toit, ich beit dich*[1]," —pleaded Evelyn, yelling, as her body twisted wildly between the sheets, her eyes sealed shut.

"Wake up, Evelyn, wake up," Vivian implored as soon as she reached her bedroom, trying to calm her terrifying, frenzied dance. "Please! I don't want to see you suffer this way!"

"What's wrong, mother? Why are you crying?" the girl asked suddenly, in a fearful tone of voice as she sat up next to her mother.

"You had another dream, but this time it was crazy—you were speaking in Yiddish!"

---

[1] I don't want to live this way anymore—without them, my world makes no sense. My God, frighten them but don't punish them with death, I beg you.

"That's impossible! How can I speak a language I don't even know?"

"I don't understand it either, sweetheart, but...the case is so serious that I think we should see a specialist who can explain what's making you get so upset."

"Dr. Colton has helped me a lot," Evelyn offered, nervously.

"I see how valuable she is, and I know she's spent hours working on your case, for years now. She also helped you overcome some of your agony and she taught you how to get along better with your classmates, and people you share things with, including Jonathan, the friend you love so much. But we're still not sure, that's why I think we have to find out where it comes from. Otherwise you'll never have the peace you need to be happy."

Perplexed, the girl reconsidered things for a moment.

"If you really think there's a way that a doctor can get rid of these horrible nightmares, well, then find him. I'm willing to cooperate in every way."

"That's what I'll do, "Vivian replied with resolve. "Now get some sleep, darling, you've got to get up early for school tomorrow. If you keep up like you have been so far, you're going to graduate with honors. I'll stay with you for a little, while you sleep, since your father's not here. He went out a couple of hours ago to attend a delivery."

"Thank you," Evelyn responded, yawning, pulling the amber-colored blanket up to her neck and lying down with her face to the wall, as she always did. "You're the very best mother in the world," she managed to say before falling into a deep sleep.

Vivian lay back on two cushions, covered in aquamarine and yellow geometrically designed cotton print, which were tied to a blond wood rocker. She remained silent, surrounded by the shadows cast on the walls by the half-light that suffused the room. She questioned herself, time and again, about her daughter's switching languages in her dreams, and the origins of those strange phrases she uttered with such inconceivable clarity.

Evelyn was a flawless birth, she said to herself, rapt in thought. The first phases of her childhood went by smoothly and happily, but when she turned five these strange occurrences started to warp her existence.

"I can't understand it—I just can't!" she exclaimed, exhausted, as she felt the warmth of thick tears clouding her vision. She waited a moment, trying to pull herself together. Scanning the walls of the room, she made out her daughter's items from childhood which where kept there by her request: The magnificent cradle specially designed and fit for the most demanding of antiques collectors, was decorated in silk and fine French lace, in shades of ecru. Her hobbyhorse, with its long, burlap mane, was finished in an array of eye-catching colors, a gift from her paternal grandparents. Her adorable ragdoll, that Vivian had very lovingly made for her, was outfitted in a cerulean-blue suit trimmed in cream-colored rick-rack, with two long flaxen braids and a perennial smile.

Tired, Vivian closed her eyes, unable to avoid the dark presentiment that unnerved her very being. Tears of anguish flowed from her eyes. It was then that Victor opened the door to Evelyn's room.

"What's the matter, darling? Why are you crying like that?" he asked nervously. Vivian got up from the rocker and gestured him to follow her. Once they left the room, she hugged him forcefully—as if her life depended on it. Calming herself for the time being, she explained to him what had happened.

"It can't be!" Victor responded incredulously. "She's never had any exposure to Yiddish. My mother spoke it when she was a girl but she never passed it on to me, much less to her granddaughter. She only tried to see if Evelyn knew certain words, and to no avail, even when you mentioned the name Duvid—the name she'd called out in some of her nightmares. All of this is so weird," he added, pensively, as he rubbed his chin.

"I'm convinced," Vivian responded anxiously, turning to look at him, "that Evelyn needs a good psychiatrist who can get to the root of this puzzle. It's inhuman to go on this way, just letting her struggle across stormy seas."

"I agree, honey. I'm going to get the ball rolling so we can find that doctor. I'll start by asking colleagues and I'll look into it at the hospital, until we find that perfect person."

After two weeks of intense searching, Victor managed to get in contact with a psychiatric specialist who had twenty-five years of uninterrupted practice, along with excellent references. Since Victor was a professional colleague at the same hospital, his request for an appointment with Dr. Carl Eidelman was immediately granted.

"Vivian, I finally found a specialist in cases like Evelyn's," Victor announced over the phone. "I bounced some ideas off him. I'll let you in on the details as soon as I get home, but in the meantime, get Evelyn ready for an appointment tomorrow at three."

"All right, darling. I'll see you tonight."

The waiting room at the medical offices of Berg, Eidelman and Freedman was crowded with patients of different backgrounds and ages. The wait traced marks of anxiety, resignation or monotony across their faces.

Three members of the Rotlewicz family went into the waiting room just as an aged and short-statured nurse called out their names. They made their way toward her.

"Good afternoon," she greeted, practically with her back to them. "Follow me, please, the doctor is expecting you."

"Come in," the psychiatrist said in tranquil tones when he heard a knock at the door. He rose from his navy blue, leather upholstered desk chair. Victor entered deliberately, followed closely by his wife and daughter.

"Thank you, Dr. Eidelman, for seeing us right away."

"I'm honored to have you here in my office," the doctor responded, extending his hand for an amicable shake. "Please be seated."

Once they all sat down, Vivian began to observe the psychiatrist's manner. He was middle aged, tall and slim, with an oval face that bore an open gaze. He had a wide, easy smile, beneath shiny, jet-black hair tinged with a hint of gray. His gestures were pleasant and resolved, evidence of a comfortable, unimpeachable background.

She breathed easily as she perceived the solidity of her husband's selection, not just in choosing the right doctor, but also for choosing a person capable of nurturing deep, compassionate feelings. She turned her attention back to the conversation the two colleagues had taken up. Victor paused briefly, then continued.

"Despite the considerable professional attention that Dr. Colton has offered my daughter in recent years, the nightmares are still happening, stronger and more often. The anxiety and pain that Evelyn's face conveys is growing more intense with time. Some dreams feature pleas and resignation, others grow violent."

"Now that I have a broad idea of the issue, I can understand the pain that you are going through, day after day," Dr. Eidelman affirmed regretfully. "But believe me when I say that if this young woman's recovery is within my power, then have no doubt about the effort and the dedication I'll put into searching out the origin of this problem. Once I've found it, I'll wipe it out at its root. I'll start with some traditional therapies but wherever possible, I'm going to try to stay away from the antidepressives that are normally used to treat anxiety and chronic fear. In most cases, these do nothing but mask the symptoms, and create a false picture of wellbeing, instead of getting at a real cure."

Chapter 8

It had been an hour and fifteen minutes since the unmistakable voice of Edgar Johnson, Professor of Architecture at Atlantic University in Boca Raton, had been heard, clearly and with precision. He enthusiastically expounded on the life, work and death of famed architect Addison Mizner.

The era and issues surrounding the subject of the lecture had captivated his audience of students. They hung on every word, their concentration intensified at key moments. All eyes were fixed on the short, portly figure of the professor: his coarse gray hair, sparsely spread across the prominent angles of his bald head that bore round spectacles resembling acrobats in constant spin. Enlightened by an ample aura of knowledge, he transferred a deep understanding of Mizner's life and work, the work of an innovative genius, whose distinctive flair applied a refined Spanish-Mediterranean lifestyle to multi-million dollar real-estate developments.

He ended the class by planting a tantalizing seed in their heads: a promise of further exploration, and the possibility that such knowledge would contribute to their future careers.

Evelyn quickly gathered the books and papers strewn about her desk. After storing them in a maroon snakeskin attaché, a gift from her boyfriend, she left the lecture hall briskly and headed to the university cafeteria for faculty and students. As soon as she entered, she eagerly scanned the room for Jonathan. He must have been waiting there for some time.

A wide smile spread across her face once she spotted him. She admired his tanned, athletic body on its notably tall frame. His square-jaw and arresting face framed by a thick mane of light brown hair.... and his amber-colored, almond-shaped eyes, both penetrating and inquisitive.

"Hey, babe!" He greeted her with an embrace.

She returned his affectionate hello.

"Sorry I'm late. Class went over and I didn't realize until it had ended. Dr. Johnson was explaining Mizner's use of Mediterranean architecture in the mansions he built at the beginning of the 1900s. It was so awesome! You really see the Spanish influence."

"You love anything about architecture, don't you? I stand before a great, famous architect of the future," Jonathan humorously declared.

"You'd better believe it, buddy," she answered with a chuckle. "But for now let's eat—I'm starving."

They finished eating and decided to walk around

campus.

"Let's sit under that big, leafy tree by the lake," Jonathan proposed after a long stretch. He pointed to a thickly trunked, ancient acacia and its tender green leaves that cast a wide shadow across the vast blue of a clear, peaceful liquid mirror.

"I want to talk to you about something," he added with some seriousness, his voice hesitant as he put his arm around her back and delicately guided her to the place he had suggested.

Once they were seated atop a spreading, cool and freshly clipped lawn, he took advantage of her proximity to embrace her tightly in his strong arms, holding her there indefinitely. He then went on to kiss her with an unbridled passion that left no doubt about his love and desires.

"I love you, Evelyn, with all my soul. Will you be my wife?" he asked her vehemently as he pulled a small jewelry box, lined in blue velvet, from his khaki-colored gabardine trousers. As the box opened, a thousand luminous reflections arose from a blue-diamond solitaire, surrounded by ten masterfully encrusted diamond chips on a white-gold Russian-style mount.

Evelyn stopped short with delight, taking in the marvelous offering. She soon noted the glint of the jewel, reflected in its lovely facets, and an intense love passed through her entire being, all thanks to this man who proposed to fulfill her most eagerly desired wish.

She parted her lips, ready to return such deep, sincere feeling, the bond that would so closely intertwine their lives, when suddenly a horrible memory arose in her mind.

"I can't marry you! I can't," she exclaimed in anguish, suddenly feeling the warmth of two thick tears that splashed down her reddened cheeks.

"But what do you mean, Evelyn? Have you gone crazy?" he asked as he lost control.

A convulsive sob kept her from answering right away. She covered her face with both hands and gave in completely to her pain as Jonathan watched her, incredulous.

"You don't understand, darling," she uttered between sobs, as she started to pull herself together following this tortuous outburst.

"Of course I don't understand," he replied angrily. "I know you love me as intensely as I love you, so why would you say no?"

She doubted for a moment as she dried her tears with a handkerchief and answered precisely.

"It's the nightmares, those terrible nightmares I told you about. I get them so often these days that they're turning my life into complete chaos."

"Honey, that doesn't matter," he offered, now calmer. "Our love can overcome any obstacle there is. We want to be together, forever—for better or for worse—and build a marriage based on staying close. I'm willing to share everything with you, including your nightmares. And I hope I can help you get rid of them completely."

"Jonathan, you're so special. And I really appreciate what you're saying. But I can't let the agony that my parents live every day spill over onto you. I love you too much to see you surrounded by that kind of pain and uncertainty. After all this time I still haven't managed to figure out the hidden messages in my dreams—but the feeling of belonging to those people, back in that time, takes complete control of me. I want to be your wife—I want it from the very deepest part of who I am. But before that can happen I need internal peace and to feel free. Otherwise I could never give myself, body and soul, to our relationship, and I doubt we would find any true happiness if that's how it were."

His head bowed, Jonathan clenched his fists in disappointment.

Recognizing his displeasure, she approached him and raised his beloved face to hers with both hands, then planted a passionate kiss on his mouth.

"Darling, please understand me and give me a chance to face this madness. Yesterday my parents and I had a special appointment with Dr. Eidelman. He explained his plans to change my course of treatment. Remember how I told you he is conservative in his professional believes but still open-minded? Well in the year and a half that I have been under observation, he has been using traditional therapies as a way of getting the most possible information from me, to determine the root factors that cause the symptoms that are masked in my nightmares. But since up to now the results have been practically nothing, he's decided to try hypnotherapy. The idea is to avoid repression and use my subconscious to search for experiences that happened when I was a girl, a teenager or in past lives, to improve my present-day life."

"I've read some scientific articles about that," he added nervously. "The process is slow and difficult and in the case of past lives, there's a lot that's still not understood."

"You're right, Jonathan. But my parents and I really believe in Dr. Eidelman, not just because he has such excellent references, but also because of how professional he has always been in past sessions."

"So you've made up your mind to go through with it?" he asked.

"Yes, sweetheart," she answered as she took him by the hand. "Right now I'm nineteen and you're twenty-three. We're young. And despite our enormous desire to join our lives as soon as possible, we should wait a reasonable time, until we can clear up this terrible mystery that traps my soul."

Chapter 9

Evelyn, following Dr. Eidelman's instructions, lay back on the maroon leather couch placed in front of the comfortably upholstered armchair, where the imposing figure of the doctor was seated. Despite innumerable explanations he had offered, she felt nervous and insecure about hypnotherapy. But she understood that through deep body relaxation she could come to enjoy more focused concentration, sharpening her memory to evoke past incidents that, masked, were affecting her life and negatively influencing her psyche, giving rise to misguided behavior patterns.

"All right, Miss Rotlewicz," she heard the doctor's hoarse voice intone, interrupting her train of thought, "to achieve a deep hypnotic state I need to be able to count on your complete cooperation. Above all you need to achieve total relaxation, and to do that, we'll begin by concentrating on your breathing.

"Please close your eyes and inhale through your

nose...hold your breath for a few seconds and then exhale, a little at a time, so that your body lets go of tensions and anxieties. Continue breathing, inhale...hold your breath and exhale, slowly. Concentrate completely on your breathing. Clear your mind of all ideas; imagine these ideas are clouds that cross the sky of your mind.

"Visualize your muscles and relax them. Relax the muscles of your face, your jaw, and your neck; continue to relax your shoulders, arms and hands. Relax your back, your hips, and your internal organs; move down to the legs, relax them, along with your feet and your toes; relax them all.

"Your entire body is relaxed and at peace. Feel gravity—your body is sinking, more and more, into the couch...

"Visualize a white light that enters your body. This light possesses an intense luminosity that enters into you slowly, very slowly, to your body's most hidden corners, relaxing every muscle, every organ, every nerve...

"Concentrate on my voice alone, blocking out every other sound that is not my voice...

"On the count of ten you will achieve greater concentration, complete relaxation and you will enter into a deep trance."

Since they had started, some twenty-two minutes had passed. Once the countdown ended there was complete silence.

Dr. Eidelman held his head in his intertwined hands and waited a few minutes before he began to speak.

"Evelyn, we will begin with the regression. To do so,

I want you to locate an important time in your childhood."

There was a pause. Then he asked, with interest: "How old are you? And where are you? Please describe everything to me in detail."

I'm eleven, she responded nervously, *and I'm in the schoolyard at the school I regularly attend. It's recess and all the students are outside the classrooms.*

I'm skipping rope. Natalie, my best friend, and Sophie, a classmate, are turning and we're taking turns jumping.

It's so much fun. As soon as I miss a jump, it's Natalie's turn… Oh, my God! I'm falling—I can't keep my balance.

My knees are bleeding! She exclaims, pained, and shifts positions on the couch to rub her injured knee. *That really hurt! It's all Natalie's fault!* She added, suddenly changing her expression from angelic to an infuriated grimace.

You let go of the rope on purpose. You wanted me to fall to get back at me for hitting you yesterday when you came to my house.

Natalie's upset, she retorted almost immediately. *She's telling me that it's not true, that I fell because I lost my balance. She swears it's not her fault.*

Is too, answers Evelyn, swinging at her.

"Stop, Evelyn," Dr. Eidelman asks her in authoritative tones, watching as she throws hard, vicious punches at the air. "Calm down and move forward a little in time," he added. "Where are you?"

I'm in Dr. Colton's office. The principal brought me

here after yelling at me and then punishing me for what happened at recess.

"I don't want a repeat of this unpleasantness," Dr. Colton is saying to me angrily. "In our last session you promised to avoid acting out and two days later you attack your best friend without pity."

I didn't mean it, Evelyn answered, sobbing. *But I couldn't help it.*

I love Natalie very much, I consider her my best friend and I can't think how my life would be if I couldn't depend on her friendship. But when I feel like I'm being picked on, I just react violently and I feel like there's this outside force that takes hold of me and pushes me to attack.

And then I'm overtaken by those horrible nightmares that I can't understand. Dr. Colton, please help me! I beg you, she added amid disconsolate crying.

"Evelyn, calm down," Dr. Eidelman beseeched her again, as he saw thick tears roll down the young woman's beautiful, delicate face. "Let's continue to go back in time. How old are you? Where are you?"

I'm eight. Day has become night and I'm in my room, in bed. My mother just put my favorite blanket on me after giving me a kiss, saying goodnight and turning out the light. I feel safe and comfortable because she decided to stay with me for a little while until I fell asleep. Daddy had to go out to see a patient who was going to have a baby and he's not back yet.

Half asleep, Evelyn heard the familiar creaking that came from the rocker; yawning, she curled her diminu-

tive form onto the couch and rolled over to face the wall.

"Move forward a little in time," the psychiatrist whispered.

Soon a horrifying scream echoed through the room.

"No! It can't be—they can't take Duvid away."

"Stay calm, Evelyn," Dr. Eidelman demanded.

They can't take Duvid away.

Duvid, darling, take me with you. Life without you—without Ariel and Ethel—has no meaning.

"Evelyn, stay calm," Dr. Eidelman insisted. "And tell me, who is Duvid?"

"My husband," she responded without hesitation.

"Who are Ariel and Ethel?" the concerned doctor asked in reply.

"They're my children—my beloved children," she answered, sobbing.

"Go back in time," he asked again. "How old are you?"

"I'm five," she replied, exhaling with excitement.

"Why are you so happy?" the doctor asked, intrigued.

I'm on the patio at my house, surrounded by toys. I just had my birthday party. My parents watched me happily and my friends have gone home.

Mother, look: my new doll is so pretty. Natalie gave it to me! She exclaimed contentedly. *I love her blue dress. But I wish her curls weren't red but golden…and with this big box of markers that Sophie gave me, now I can color everything I want! And look, Daddy, at this dress that's so pretty…it's my favorite color…grandma gave it to me so I can wear it to the birthday party that my school friend Raul's mom and dad are going to have for him. But I'm so thirsty!* The little girl exclaimed as she made a playful pout.

"I'm going to bring you a glass of orange juice, sweetheart," my mother says as she gets up." I'll bet you've eaten too much cake at the party."

"I'll come with you," my father added, following after her. Fascinated, I keep gazing at all the toys spread out around me on the rug covering a part of the stones that make up an extensive lanai. Every so often I look up to take in a dazzling glow that comes from intense sunlight, reflected in the huge pool's blue and crystalline waters. It is shaded by abundant palms that sway to the rhythm of warm breezes, surrounded by an equal number of tall grasses grouped with the palms that create a sort of protective wall.

I'm tired of keeping my legs crossed for so long, she said, stretching them out and raising her head in a lazy gesture, extending her arms to move her bodyweight from hands that are resting on the floor.

Suddenly, there's a wave of distress in her face. Something strange is happening around her. The bright, relaxing atmosphere, so familiar, has transformed into a queer, depressing panorama. The sky darkens; ghostly gray buildings, terribly run down, spring up all around; dusty streets, ill kept, lead from here to there, glacially cold and menacing. Shaken, Evelyn was about to shout out to her parents but she stopped herself when she saw a little boy, nearly the same age as she, and a younger little girl that were coming over to her in slow, shaky strides. Their gazes reflected a chilling fear; their malnourished bodies were covered in what were truly tatters that hung from them, saturated in filth and stench.

Do you want to play with my new toys and me? She asks them sympathetically, repressing her growing fear at these wretched creatures' appearance.

"Mama, mama!" the two children shout in unison, extending their skeletal arms toward me.

My mom went to the kitchen for a while, but she's coming back soon, she responds with an innocent air.

"Mama, mama," they continue to beg, staring at me, their eyes clouded over with thick tears that stream down their sunken, wilted faces.

I told you mother was coming back soon, Evelyn shouts, terrified.

"Honey, what's wrong?" my mother asks, worried. She heard my cries and tries to restore balance to a tray bearing three glasses of orange juice that threatened to fall in reaction to her haste.

Those kids don't want to play with me. They won't stop crying and they're asking for their mother, she answered, fleeing to her mother's side.

"What children?" she asks confusedly.

Evelyn let go of her mother's skirt, turned physically and extended her arm to point out exactly where the two wraiths were. To her surprise, her surroundings had reassumed their original form and there was no trace of the children's existence.

They were here until you came! The girl exclaimed,

confused. The pool went away and there were these tall, dirty buildings and torn-up streets that they were walking on. They were dressed weird and they wouldn't stop crying and asking for their mother.

Papa was able to hear my last description and he furrowed his brow. He addressed Mother hoarsely.

"I think today has been too much for her. You should give her a hot bath, feed her dinner and put her to bed."

"You're entirely right, honey. That's just what I'm going to do," she responded with concern.

"Move forward to that very night," the doctor said in a trembling tone of voice.

Evelyn curled up on the couch, turned to the wall and shut her eyes.

The doctor looked away from the body that was lying there, and with his right hand brushed back a lock of hair that had accidently fallen across his wide forehead. He changed position in an effort to better settle into his armchair. It had been a hard day and he thought to end the session soon.

Suddenly a horrifying shout was heard, breaking the surrounding silence and sending the psychiatrist's heart racing at a terrible rate. It took him a second or two to pull himself together after the shock he'd received.

They're taking him away…they're taking him away and I'll never know anything about him and my children again, he heard her wail desperately. *Till now no one has ever been able to come back from where he's going, and we don't know what will happen. I'm going to look for him right now! Later there won't be time*, she said resolutely as she sprung from the couch and tried to run away.

But a strange force held her back, impeding any advance.

"What's happening, Evelyn?" asked Dr. Eidelman with consternation.

There's a woman near me who won't let me go. She's holding my arm, she says I have no right to risk my life this way, She doesn't understand that life has no meaning for me if I can't be with the people I love.

Let me go! Evelyn shouted hysterically, trying to remove her trapped arm. *Please! Let me go… Let me go…*

Chapter 10

The wedding march's sublime notes floated up from the instruments the Manolo Zoyla Orchestra played, then burst into the room and seized the attention of three hundred fifty guests there present.

Evelyn advanced down the aisle with slow, precise steps, dressed in a vaporous hazelnut-colored dress; her long, lustrous hair was pulled back by delicate, diamond-covered clips that matched a heart-shaped pendant that hung from her neck by a golden chain, a gift from her parents. Holding a round bouquet of delicate pink and white roses, set off by fern and eucalyptus, she advanced gracefully and deliberately along the pathway set off by yards of cream-colored tulle and hundreds of fragrant, multi-colored flowers.

Soon Natalie appeared, dressed in white, in a magnificent headdress embroidered in iridescent sequins, especially designed for the occasion. A transparent veil covered her face yet did nothing to mask the extraordinary glimmer of her eyes or her ever-present smile, reflecting intense happiness within her. Both parents, advancing with her on either side, led her to the altar to wed Mauricio Goldberg, the man of her dreams.

Jonathan, seated among the guests, watched intently as the bridal party passed. When he saw the groom walk halfway down the aisle to receive the beautiful bride from her parents, he was overcome by mixed emotions.

He rejoiced in the happiness it augured for his friends. Yet his most fervent wish, to make Evelyn his bride, was growing more difficult by the day.

Intense months of therapy had not been able to mitigate his girlfriend's overwhelming anxieties. Nightmares and terrible daydreams continued as harsh as ever, preventing her from making important life decisions despite the deep love that united the two young people.

"I love you, darling, more than I love my own life," Jonathan whispered into Evelyn's ear as he held her tightly in his arms and they danced to the rhythm of the *Blue Danube Waltz.*

"And I adore you," she answered, filled with emotions. "You'll never completely understand how intensely I feel," she said, stepping back slightly to look into his eyes.

"Then agree to marry me," he pleaded.

"Jonathan, I can't. I've explained it to you a thousand times. I need to know what's causing my problems, those terrible nightmares that keep me from sleeping. Sometimes when I'm alone, I wonder if I'm not mad for imagining all this. But it is so real, so all-consuming...

watching my life from the outside; you'd think everything was normal. There's you, my parents, my work...these incredible moments of happiness," she added as two thick tears slid down her delicate face.

"Please don't cry," he begged her. "I wish I could take all the anguish from your life—or at least that you'd let me share it with you. But you'd better believe we're going to get to the bottom of this. And soon we'll build a home filled with peace and happiness where the past is forgotten."

The following week Victor Rotlewicz was shaking hands with his colleague Dr. Eidelman, just minutes after reaching the latter's office.

"Thanks for getting back to me so soon," Dr. Eidelman said, pointing him to the seat nearest his desk.

"I need to speak to you before we go on with your daughter's treatment."

Victor sat down silently and waited for him to go on.

"In previous discussions that we've had, and based on the reports I've been sending you each month, you can surmise that therapeutic outcomes have not presented solutions equal to the depth of the problem we've been facing. When I decided to use hypnotherapy as a support instrument, I believed I would be able to uproot many of the problems behind her affliction. Now fourteen months of frustrations have passed and, seeing the negligible advances we've been able to make, I decided to ask your permission to try a more aggressive method. I'd like," he added with some hesitation, "to begin past-life regression therapy with Evelyn."

"What are you talking about?" Victor asked, getting up from his chair.

"Take it easy, my friend—and please have a seat," Dr. Eidelman entreated, pushing back a silvery lock of hair that had fallen carelessly across his wide forehead.

Victor fell back onto his seat, upset, staring straight at the psychiatrist, not knowing what to say.

"The notion of regression sounds shady to non-professionals. But more and more psychiatrists and hypnotists are incorporating it into their practice, for cases that are exceedingly complex or impossible to solve using just traditional hypnotherapy, based on the patient's current life. Over time, the number of people who believe in multiple lives has increased. These lives offer individuals a variety of lessons that are needed for them to overcome problems of the soul.

"A number of controversial doctors, utterly opposed to accepting this theory, have been surprised by what has emerged in hypnotic sessions, where they have asked patients to return to the moment when the symptoms causing their problems began. Suddenly they find themselves talking with an entirely different person, whose name, sex, or even the place where they are or the time in which they say they are living differ completely from current realities.

"You should keep in mind that I am not in the habit of using this method, except in specific cases that require it. But I have no doubt that your daughter's case is one of these."

"In that case let's move forward," Victor responded

resolutely. "I have complete confidence in you, both as a friend and a professional. My daughter couldn't be in better hands."

Chapter 11

Evelyn laid back on Dr. Eidelman's maroon leather couch with her head on a soft pillow in a white case. Dressed in a royal blue *crepe-de-chine* outfit gathered at both sides of her figure, her eyes closed, she seemed to be napping. In fact she was in a state of complete concentration, carried away by the psychiatrist's melodious voice that, during months of therapy, had won its patient's entire trust and had in just a short time placed her into a deep state of hypnosis.

"Now, Miss Rotlewicz," the doctor asked slowly, "I need you to go back in time to the moment when the causes of your nightmares began."

There was an immediate change in the young woman's peaceful expression.

He waited a few minutes and then asked her curiously, "Evelyn, what's happening? Explain everything to me, in complete detail."

Suddenly she began to describe the atmosphere

surrounding her, in Yiddish.

"No, Evelyn, not in Yiddish. Talk to me in English," said the doctor somewhat nervously.

My name is not Evelyn—don't call me that, she responded in anger. *My name is Bluma Feldman, I'm twelve years old, and an only child of Isaac and Jaika Feldman. I'm having lunch now, in the dining room at home, with my parents. Having them near makes me feel safe and protected. But papa doesn't like too much talk when we eat. He's a grocer and he's done very well in the business. My mama takes care of everything about my education and minding the house.*

"Where are you and what year is it?" asked the doctor curiously, after snapping his fingers.

I am in Iwaniska, a town in Poland. It's 1923.

"Move forward ten years to an important date," requested Dr. Eidelman with authority.

Today is the twelfth of September 1933, a day that I'll never be able to forget. Rabbi Rabinowicz just married Duvid Zonchtein and me in the synagogue we normally attend, under a chuppah adorned with a Star of David, covered in beautiful, multicolored flowers.

We're headed to my parents' house. They're hosting a party for us. We're happy to be together even if they arranged the marriage. We learned to love and respect one another, and I hope it will be that way for the rest of our lives.

"Move ahead once more to another important date," he asked.

Our first child has been born. He's a strong, healthy

boy that we've been expecting anxiously in recent months. The doctor just pulled him from my body and I can hear his strong screams. I can feel his presence on my breast, where they've placed him right this minute. An intense emotion has come over me.

My God! I never thought I could feel such love. It's a different feeling than any other I've ever experienced—even than what I feel for my husband and my parents—something very profound and special. We have decided to call him Ariel in honor of Duvid's father. That was his name when he was alive, but he died two years ago, leaving an intense void in all of our lives. He was a disciplined man, full of wisdom, and a real role model for everyone around him.

"Bluma, did you have other children?" the psychiatrist asked, intrigued.

Yes, a beautiful little girl who was born a year after Ariel. We called her Ethel, in honor of my maternal grandmother, may she rest in peace.

"Talk to me a little about your family life," Dr. Eidelman asked.

We live in a comfortable house with two bedrooms, a wedding gift from my parents. It's built of wood and painted olive green. The windows have long window boxes filled with brightly colored geraniums. The garden isn't big, but it is attractive, surrounded by hundred-year-old trees with thick trunks. All kinds of birds come to perch in their branches. An endless variety of plants surround them and Duvid, the children and I could not enjoy it more. There's a strong loving bond between us—we feel happy to be together and to share our life with such special children. We have watched them grow up healthy and strong, surrounded by family, neighbors and friends with whom we celebrate holidays and our culture's traditions.

We are Jews and we belong to a community whose spiritual and cultural richness makes us proud. My people come from many different countries around the world. It has led to an intermingling of countless ideas, customs and languages. We offer a good education to our children and in the near future, if possible, we would like to move to Warsaw or Cracow, where there are yeshivas, grand synagogues, theatres, and important, world-renowned people in the realms of music, literature, science and philosophy. In short, we have a peaceful, happy life.

Sometimes Duvid criticizes my misbehavior, a product of the excessive affection my parents gave me when I was a girl, but he knows my soul deep down and also knows that goodness and love are the raw materials of my existence.

"Let's go forward in time once more."

Oh, no, she responded nervously.

"What is it, Bluma?" asked the psychiatrist, observing his patient's aggrieved face.

A neurasthenic madman named Hitler has been giving speeches in Germany with an emphasis on the "master race," meaning that Germans are the prototype of the Superman, demeaning the rest of humanity. This is a threat—a terrible threat!

"Why do you think so?" asked Dr. Eidelman, encouraging her to speak more.

I've always known that the differences between races, religions and nationalities create antagonism between human beings, and we, as Jews, have lived that all our lives. Our relationship with the Poles has been one of simple tolerance and convenience, but at root there is a feeling of hate and jealousy.

But now—inflamed by this individual, overflowing with hate and without scruples, who was raised in the heart of a home and a religion that warped his child's mind and saturated him in principles and prejudices based on erroneous facts and events, who spreads ideas against the Jewish religion, and given that his life has never been successful—I feel like the near future for everyone who is not German will be filled with pain.

"Move forward in time and tell me what year it is."

It's 1939 and we are going through intensely anguished, painful times. Trucks filled with Nazi soldiers, sent by Hitler and his followers, reach our neighborhood daily, ordered to haul off anyone they believe to be of an inferior race. We've seen entire blocks of old people, men, women and children disappear, hurried out of their houses, mercilessly pushed and mistreated by cruel soldiers who only allow them to carry a few belongings with them, forcing them to get into trucks by beating them with the butts of their rifles. We never hear from them again.

"Where do you think they are being taken?" asks the doctor, intrigued.

We've heard different theories. Some people think they're taken somewhere where they have to do forced labor, others think they want to confiscate their property without paying indemnities. However most of the neighbors have heard alarming rumors from people who have managed to escape from concentration camps, and they insist that no one who gets arrested gets out alive, since Hitler's most burning desire is to take over the entire world, and because of the deep-seated hate he feels for any nationality that is not German—especially the Jews.

"Bluma, now I want you to go forward a few months to an important date in your life," asks Carl Eidelman with a deeply pained expression.

It's May 4th, 1939. Duvid, the children and I are seated around the dining room table in our house. We are there with two older people of whom we are very fond: Morris and Tamara Ianovsky. They set up a clandestine printing press in the basement of their house where they run off and distribute the latest war news.

We visit them often for long conversations that we quite enjoy and when we're with them we usually learn a thousand new things. They are people with deeply human values and over time we have come to consider them dear friends despite the differences in our ages. Ariel and Ethel love them as they would love their own grandparents.

She paused and withdrew into herself.

"Keep on with your story, Bluma," asked the doctor after a few minutes had passed.

The dinner ended a few hours ago and the children

are asleep in their room. Duvid and I just went to bed and despite how late it is I can't sleep from enjoying all the incredible stories that Morris just told us. It's true that knowledge comes with the passage of time.

But what's that? There are loud knocks at the front door. "Duvid, Duvid, wake up."

"What is it, Bluma? Why are you waking me up?"

"Don't you hear that knocking?"

"Oh, dear God. Please let it not be the Germans," exclaimed Duvid as he bolted upright.

"Please, don't answer the door—maybe they'll go away."

"If we don't open up they'll knock it down," he added as he made his way to the entrance.

"You are to come with us," shouted a Nazi in a green uniform and high, black patent-leather boots. You have five minutes to gather any belongings. Schnell, schnell.*"*

"Bluma, run wake up the children and let's get dressed right away. We shouldn't resist. I've seen how one of them beat one of our neighbors with the butt of his rifle and the neighbor nearly lost an eye."

"Ariel, Ethel... wake up."

"What is it, mother?"

"Get dressed quickly and come with us."

"But it's night. Where are we going? I'm too tired," Ethel answered, whining.

"No questions and hurry it up," Duvid responded authoritatively.

"Schnell, schnell,*" the German continued to shout.*

"Get into the truck immediately," another soldier

brusquely demanded as soon as he saw them carrying a small suitcase, a silver candelabrum, the girl's favorite teddy bear and a storybook.

"Mama, I'm scared," Ariel added, confused, as Ethel continued to pout.

"Let's do what they say," said Bluma, worried, helping them up into the truck.

Surprised to recognize several people from the neighborhood there, they filed to the rear of the truck and sat on the floor, numbed more by fear than by cold.

The Nazi soldiers closed the rear door of the truck and the roundup continued, stopping at a number of nearby residences where the procedure was repeated; in some cases where there was resistance, the consequences were terrible. The Germans had no tolerance for any form of rebellion.

The silence inside the truck was absolute. No one dared speak a word, but their faces reflected intense anguish and desperation in light of an uncertain future.

"They're going to kill us!" said an old man between sobs, covering his eyes in mortification. He was seated next to Duvid.

"Don't say that!" Bluma quickly responded.

"I assure you it will happen," the old man said, removing his hands from his face and blowing his nose.

"How can you be so certain?" a young man seated in front of him asked. He held his wife's hand steadily.

"I understand German and in the brief time those bastards gave me to gather my things, I was able to overhear them. They said, laughing, that each person's

death—especially the death of every Jew—helped realize the Fuhrer's eagerly held desire to get rid of anyone who didn't share his beliefs, or look like them, from the face of the earth. That will empower them to grow. "

"What can we do to save our children from such a miserable end?" Bluma asked desperately."

"I don't know," answered the old man, saddened. "At my age, it's to be expected that death come calling, but the children...what awaits them isn't right."

"Dear God, don't allow this to happen!" Bluma cried out, horrified. "Don't let this happen, please!"

The truck continued along the narrow path bordered by wood-frame houses. The night was calm, dressed in a full moon and numerous twinkling stars. Suddenly they felt a brusque movement and the vehicle stopped. Then they heard the soldiers' voices in alarmed tones.

"What are they saying?" Duvid asked the old man anxiously.

"It looks like the truck has some kind of mechanical problem and we have to wait until they repair it," he responded softly.

"Look where we are, Duvid," said Bluma in her husband's ear.

"In front of the Ianovskys' house," he added as he stared back at her.

"Are you thinking what I am?" she asked him nervously.

He answered with an affirmative nod.

"So let's do it," she answered with resolve.

Bluma got as close as she could to Ariel and whis-

pered into his ear. "Sweetheart, take your little sister's hand and without saying a word, go with her to the Ianovskys' house. Your father and I will help you get down but do not let the soldiers see you. It's night and that's a help; hide in the weeds if you need to. And, you, little girl, promise me that you'll follow Ariel wherever he takes you and that you won't say a word until you're inside their house."

"I promise, mama," Ethel answered very formally, raising her little hand in a gesture of agreement.

Bluma and Duvid hugged them quickly and then took them by the hand to walk to the rear of the truck. Once they were there, they helped the children slip silently away until they let go of their parents' hands and reached the ground with a hop, conscious that the Germans were distracted at the front of the truck trying to figure out what was wrong with the motor.

Ariel ran forward, dragging his sister by the hand as their parents anxiously watched the little children's maneuver.

The last sight they had of their children was when they saw them cross toward the courtyard; then their figures disappeared into the darkness.

Ariel headed toward the back door of the house, off the courtyard, and they went through it silently, obeying their mother's instructions.

Both Duvid and Bluma and those near them breathed a sigh of relief when they saw the Germans hadn't seen what happened. Some minutes later they heard the sound of the motor and the truck lurched for-

ward.

Dr. Eidelman pulled a white handkerchief from his pants pocket to wipe the sweat that had beaded on his brow. The tension of his patient's painful experiences had been too much for him and he decided to close the session.

"Bluma, at the count of ten you will awaken and feel an intense inner peace."

Chapter 12

"Oh my God, what have I done?" shouted Bluma in consternation.

"What are you talking about?" asked Duvid anxiously when he saw her in such a desperate state.

"We've just left our children in Morris and Tamara Ianovsky's care, without stopping to think that they are Jews just like us; the most likely thing is that maybe in just a few days the Nazis will come for them. Then what will happen? How will we find them later?"

Duvid watched her, frozen and silent. What had happened had happened so quickly that they'd had no time to consider the consequences of their actions. Now it was too late; they couldn't bring back their children. Just the thought of it made him tremble.

He tightly embraced his wife and they cried out their desperation together at length, until exhaustion overcame them, and they fell asleep surrounded by others overwhelmed by their uncertain fate.

"Go on with your story." Dr. Eidelman requested after a few minutes of silence had passed.

The morning light awakened us. I feel like my heart has been shredded with pain and there's an intense void in my soul. How can I live without my children? How can I live down the guilt of having abandoned them?

"Please, Bluma, don't cry," Duvid begged, seeing her eyes filled with tears, knowing the intense pain her pupils reflected.

"Good God, what are we going to do?" she wondered, letting loose with a sudden burst of sobbing.

"I don't know," Duvid replied, with a sharp stab to the heart. "I don't know," he repeated to himself. "I don't know!"

The truck continued on its way, then stopped after a long bounce. The front door opened and two Nazis got out. They briskly made their way to the rear of the vehicle and rapidly opened the door.

"Schnell, schnell—*get moving and get out of the truck!" shouted one fiercely countenanced Nazi.*

"Go on, Bluma," requested the psychiatrist.

She waited a few minutes before continuing. Her face bore the marks of intense sorrow and curiosity.

We're in the train station and there are all these people. It seems more like a market than a place for transportation. People are running around frantically, looking for family members, trying to hold on to belongings and at the same time seeking to avoid assaults on the part of the Germans who shove and injure at the slightest provocation. Holding hands, Duvid and I are fol-

lowing the line of people that got out of the truck with us.

The Nazis are moving us toward a boxcar, seemingly made for animals, not human beings. There is a pregnant woman ahead of us that seems ready to give birth, exhausted, and several times has nearly collapsed. Men, women and children bear shadowy faces. Some cry, others cry out, and others say nothing.

Everything is chaotic—a horrible nightmare.

Now we are within the boxcar. We've been pushed to the rear where there are no windows. Numerous people continue to board; the air grows dense and we cannot sit down since there are few empty seats. The Germans keep filling the car and we feel packed in against the others.

I stick right by Duvid and I'm terribly frightened—not only for what is happening but fearful for what will happen to our children, now stripped of our protection and help.

How could I have committed such a heinous act of abandonment? How could a mother behave that way? God will not forgive me; I deserve anything that happens to me.

"Bluma, don't stop there—please go on," asked Dr. Eidelman, since what she was saying was beginning to shed some light on the problem that had so affected Evelyn's life.

We've just heard a loud, crackling noise. The Germans have shut the boxcar door, securing it from the outside so that no one can escape. But God! They're plugging the breathing holes. How will we survive?

"Bluma, move forward in time to the train's arrival," the psychiatrist asked anxiously, to avoid hearing about all the suffering and death that came from the inhuman conditions that the Nazis imposed on so many millions.

The train has stopped, but for us it's all the same: the darkness, the cries, the lack of air and the stench of the boxcar has left a permanent wound in our lives. We've been treated worse than savage beasts, humiliated, demeaned and stripped of our self-respect. They are opening the door and I can feel the air penetrate inside; I breathe deeply and let my eyes grow accustomed to the light. I focus my vision. Good God, what a scene of horror.

Live human beings lean against inert bodies, redolent of putrefaction, and there is wailing all about and then the sudden cry of a little baby. I turn and there is the little child in his dead mother's arms; I stir and relax my iron grip on Duvid's hand, and with what little strength I have left, I pick up the little body and carry it with me.

"Look, Duvid, it's a newborn baby," I say, moved.

He looks at me with melancholy eyes that bring to mind my own children and an unwitting tear wells up in my eye.

"Schnell, schnell—*get down from the car," the Nazi bastards shout at the top of their lungs, emboldened by their power.*

Thus begins the wretched descent, stepping atop people that did not survive the scabrous journey. Duvid helps me get up from the ground as I envelop the baby's warm little body in my arms, to keep from dropping it, and we hurry from the car as if by doing such a thing we could erase all that has happened.

The light disorients us for a moment and as soon as we adjust we see the place and we understand that we've reached our destination: Auschwitz.

"Line up, line up," we hear uniformed men shout, carrying fearsome weapons they used without compulsion, wherever needed, to control the crowds.

"Women to the right, men to the left!"

"Oh, no, Duvid, they're going to separate us!"

"I won't let them—not that."

But as they advanced they understood that sticking together was going to be impossible. They tightly embraced, each trying to take the other's essence with him.

"I love you, darling," Duvid said to her as he felt a Nazi forcibly tear him from his wife's side as she, holding tightly to the infant, stood paralyzed by pain.

"Come with me, madam, if you wish not to be mistreated by these Nazi perverts" said a young woman who spoke with a Romanian accent.

Bluma nodded and let her lead her away, feeling that what little strength she still had was leaving her.

The long wait in lines, the hose-down, having heads shaved, changing into the camp uniform—all happened without any awareness on her part. Her mind was paralyzed by the memory of Duvid and her children.

That night, installed in her barracks, she began to react.

"Where's the baby?" she questioned worriedly.

Sasha, the Romanian girl that had been helping her

all day, lowered her voice as she answered.

"He's dead. He couldn't survive without food and apparently he hadn't eaten since he'd been born. I didn't have anything to give him. The Germans carried off his lifeless body."

Bluma nodded and closed her eyes, letting sleep carry her off to a different world.

Chapter 13

Dr. Eidelman settled into his chair, waiting for his patient to begin speaking after quickly inducing a state of hypnosis in her.

Bluma opened her eyes suddenly and sat up amid all the noise her barrack-mates were making.

"What's happening?" she worriedly asked Sasha, the Romanian girl, who was next to her at the time.

Before receiving an answer they heard a loud blow, the door opened with a clatter, and several Nazis entered.

"Schnell, schnell—*get out right away—it's time to work. This is not a hotel, move quickly!" A German shouted orders, waving his rifle about menacingly.*

Her heart racing, Bluma got down from her blanketless wood bunk and without even stretching her aching muscles, she went out in silence. Outside the temperature had dropped from what it was the day before. Bluma didn't think it strange; winter was coming and wrapped only in the camp uniform the Germans had given her when she'd arrived on the train, she could not get warm.

She looked up at the heavens and guessed it was five in the morning, but she couldn't confirm it since they had confiscated her wristwatch as soon as they had started the "cleaning" process.

The shouting kept up. She understood a few words in German because of its resemblance to Yiddish and she surmised the guards were explaining the rules of the camp, to be immediately adhered to.

She carefully studied the line of women standing there shivering from the chill of such an early hour. The line extended in both directions from where she stood, and she could see that the Germans were there to exterminate all those people brought from various concentration camps in nations all over Europe. Their unwavering idea was to prevent anyone from standing in the way of Hitler, their Führer's, *most eagerly coveted dream: conquering the world.*

Once the ghoulish-looking Nazi had finished his explanation, it was time to divide up the work and Bluma, accompanied by other female inmates, Sasha included, were put to work collecting items confiscated from each person who got off the trains, to be put into big bags and sent to Germany.

Well, thanks to this work, Bluma thought, relieved, I'll be able to watch the trains' arrival up close and maybe I'll even spot my children.

All day long they collected garments, watches, false teeth, shoes, money, candelabras, silverware, toys, or-

thopedic devices, suitcases, jewels and whole series of objects the people that got off the trains had brought with them, hoping to retain the scant possessions they had been allowed to take in one suitcase. But these were confiscated as soon as they arrived.

Day after day the process continued, and at night, with their feet swollen, their bodies freezing and a deep sense of anguish in their souls, the prisoners would lie down near to one another hoping to muster up some heat and keep the diseases that insistently hovered around the barracks at bay.

"I haven't been able to find my children. I can't find them," Bluma repeated in her desperation. "What happened to them? Where did it all end? Dear God, return them to me soon. Make all this nothing more than some terrible nightmare. And what of Duvid? Is he still alive or did they kill him? It can't be true—he's young and still full of life.

"The Nazis know how to pick out the ones who can work and offer them privileges; I'm sure Duvid will survive. He's probably looking for Ariel just as I'm searching for Ethel. We're going to find them."

"Move forward in time to an important event," the doctor asked as he observed an intense pain afflict his patient.

"It's Tamara Ianofsky! She's getting off the train," Bluma exclaimed excitedly. "Tamara! Tamara!"

"Take it easy," Sasha pleaded, seizing her arm to keep her from dashing off. "If the Nazis hear you they'll kill you right on the spot".

"But you don't understand, I'm finally going to see the woman who's been taking care of my children for the last five months."

"Let's keep putting things into the bags and that way we'll try to get close to her, so the Nazis don't suspect that there's something up with you."

"But I can never lose sight of her," Bluma added, nervously.

"That won't happen if we proceed with caution," Sasha replied immediately. Little by little they got closer to her.

"Tamara. Tamara." She heard a familiar voice call her by her first name. She turned her head to follow the sound and suddenly found herself face-to-face with her beloved friend Bluma. They embraced forcefully and the emotion was so intense that tears burst from their eyes.

She stood back a bit, to see her better, and her face reflected the pain she felt seeing her friend's own emaciated expression. Her figure was gaunt from hunger and too much work and even more, she perceived Bluma's intense worry about the three beings that were her entire life.

"Dear girl, what have they done to you?" she asked, taken aback.

"Where are my children, Tamara, why aren't they with you?"

"Your children are safe," she answered immediately.

"Thank God they're all right! But where are they?" she asked again.

"The night the children reached our house, Morris

and I were afraid the Nazis would soon show up to deport us, so we decided to call our friend Abel Goldstein, a key figure in the Jewish resistance who was being hidden in a Catholic friend's house. Despite the danger that having Abel there meant, they had decided to help them, too.

"With his influence we were able to smuggle the children out of the ghetto, by digging a hole beneath the surrounding brick wall. There were three people that Abel had designated waiting on the other side who agreed to take them someplace out of danger.

"Two weeks later we found out the children had traveled to France accompanied by a representative of the French Consulate who pretended they were his own for the duration of the trip. Once they reached France he took them to the 'Maison Izieu,' a children's summer camp. They're there with forty-two other children and nine teachers, which make me think it would be a good place for them to stay safe until the war ends.

"In the meantime, Morris and I stayed on top of their progress. They were happy in the camp but they missed you both the whole time."

"Oh my poor little babies," Bluma sighed tenderly.

"Get moving, schnell, schnell,*" barked a furious Nazi when he saw the trio of women speaking to one another.*

"No, please don't take her away," Bluma, exclaimed in desperation. She suddenly felt a forceful blow that caused her to lose consciousness.

When she came to, she was lying on a bunk in the barracks. Her head hurt intensely and when she touched it she discovered an open wound that bled.

"Sasha, what happened?" she asked, perplexed, not understanding the situation.

"That Nazi bastard hit you so hard in the head you passed out. You've been delirious for three days straight."

"Now I remember I was talking to Tamara... But, where is she?" Bluma asked as she struggled to sit up. "I need her to tell me where my children are."

Sasha looked on regretfully, holding her down to keep her from getting out of the bunk. It was still too soon. She'd let a few days pass before explaining what happened.

"Let's move forward in time," the doctor asked, anxious to know what had passed.

"Sasha, it just can't be," Bluma exclaimed amid her sobs. "They can't have carried her off to the gas chambers. I have to know where my children are and what's happened to them. And Tamara was such a good person. How could they have killed her that way? They're murderers—sick, filthy murderers!" she screamed with fury.

Carl Eidelman lowered his head and covered his face with the palms of his hands, unable to hear any more about the cruelty and cynicism his patient had been a victim of.

As a doctor, he was used to hearing sad, painful stories. But what Evelyn was describing just then was soul crushing.

How could human beings act with such cruelty? Was

there no such thing as pity and compassion?

As he pulled himself together, he decided to end the session. He finally understood why his patient suffered from those horrible nightmares that went on and on, preventing her from enjoying a normal existence. It was time to make a definitive move and he would guide her through whatever it took to put the reins of her own life back into her hands.

Chapter 14

Abraham Rotlewicz stepped down from his Bentley quickly and made his way to the front door of his son Victor's house, then rang the doorbell.

The family meeting was at three in the afternoon and it was already 4:15.

He cordially greeted the housekeeper who opened the door and made his way to the living room.

"Sorry to be late," he excused himself. "There was a last-minute meeting I couldn't get out of."

"Don't worry, Dad," said Victor, rising from the sofa and approaching him with an affectionate embrace. "Sit here next to mom," he invited, pointing to a seat. "Can I get you a whiskey and soda?"

"Thanks, son, I'd appreciate that," he replied immediately, as he sat down next to his wife, with a kiss. "Where's Vivian?" he asked, surprised not to see her.

"She'll be back in a minute," Lea answered. "While we were waiting for you she went to the kitchen to tell the cook how she wants dinner done."

"There you are, Dad," said Victor as he handed over the whiskey.

"Thanks."

"Hello there, Mr. Abraham," Vivian greeted as she came into the room. She approached her father-in-law and kissed him on the cheek.

"How's my favorite daughter-in-law?"

"Well, a little busy—but good, thank you."

"Mom, dad…" Victor began to speak. "We asked you to come over and meet with us so that we could bring you up to date on the conclusions that Dr. Eidelman has come to, after all these extended therapy sessions that Evelyn has been going through. We truly believe they've been quite beneficial to her."

Attentive to what was being said, Abraham and Lea urged Victor to go on.

"As you already are aware, Evelyn's nightmares have been coming back every day, more frequently and intensely, and have overwhelmed her with doubts and anxieties. As a result, she hasn't been willing—or able—to follow the normal path that a person her age might. That's how her relationship with Jonathan is. He is such a great young man, in love with her—in every sense of the word—and he's ready to get married.

"Yet Evelyn has the impression that because of her nightmares, she's already caused her family too much pain. She feels that her love for Jonathan is so deep that there's nothing in the world that would make her expose him to so much suffering and instability."

"What are you thinking of doing?" Lea intervened.

"Dr. Eidelman suggests that Evelyn must confront the past," Victor quickly explained, "to discover the roots of the problem that is tearing her apart in all these gruesome nightmares."

"But Victor—," Vivian interrupted, surprised, "I don't understand how our daughter can search for a solution to her problem in a past that isn't even hers...that comes from we don't know where... and for reasons we can't understand."

"Look at it this way, dear," Victor answered patiently. "Like we said before, what's happening in Evelyn's nightmares is tied up with one of her past lives, something that couldn't be resolved during the span of that life...and that has had a tremendous impact on her being. Can you imagine the pain of losing two children that way, without being able to ever see them again, without knowing what was their fate? Did they survive or did the Nazis exterminate them? What about the husband? Did he die? Did he live? Did he look for her when the war ended? What happened? Everything in that life went unanswered.

"Years later, our daughter was born and grew up in an atmosphere of love, peace and economic security, but her soul retained the scars from the devastating pain of losing those who were most beloved to her. As time went on and she grew older, just the idea of living with that uncertainty became intolerable to her.

"That's why I asked to meet today, to let you know that I've decided to offer Evelyn all the support necessary to clear things up in her life. I'm going to give her whatever she needs to make that happen.

"I hope, Vivian, I can count on your approval and help; and this is what I'm asking of my own parents, since I consider them our closest connection."

Vivian went to him, embraced him tightly, and then said with some emotion:

"Thank you, darling, for being the man you are. Of course I'll do everything within reach to make sure Evelyn gets to the bottom of these nightmares."

"You can count on us for anything that's needed," Abraham added right away.

"Thank you. I didn't expect anything less from the two of you," Victor responded emotionally.

"And now I'll tell you about the plan we're going to follow," Victor commented with a pause before going on. "The idea is to send Evelyn to Poland—specifically to Ivansk, or Iwaniska as the Poles call it—the town that she mentions in her nightmares, and once she's there, let her do a deep investigation of whatever issues she needs to soothe the emotions that are now overwhelming her with anguish."

He took a deep breath and went on. "Sadly, with my work and my patients, I won't be able to go with her. I'd have liked to—"

"I want to go with her," Lea called out.

Everyone turned to look at her, incredulous.

"But, mother—," Victor responded immediately. "Are you sure you want to return to Poland after all the traumatic things you had to face there?"

"Yes, son," she answered resolutely. "I want with all my heart to go with my granddaughter on her journey, to help her find the mental peace she desperately needs—it will help me face the truth, too."

Chapter 15

The airplane took off with a tremendous roar from the runway at Miami International airport, making a series of precise movements, and then straightening its course to the east.

Lea and Evelyn each settled into their seats, said nothing as they remembered goodbyes and innumerable recommendations family and friends had made.

Now the trip was a reality and each woman's mind overflowed with thoughts about immense possibilities and uncertainties.

"Jonathan, darling," Evelyn thought, "I'm going to be far away from you; I'm going to miss you so much. I hope soon we'll achieve the results we're expecting and be together again."

"God, give me the strength I need at times like these, to face the ghosts of the past," Lea implored, softly, gazing out the airplane window at the darkness that ruled the night, save for several tiny stars the plane left behind as it continued on its course.

Hours passed inexorably as the women dozed in and out. The next day announced its presence by flooding the jet with the dawn's first rays, filtered through the window's thick transparency and caressing the passengers' slumbering faces.

"Good morning little girl," said Lea as she saw Evelyn open her eyes.

"Wow, I slept well!" she immediately exclaimed, rubbing her eyes and seeking to shy away from the intense light assaulting her pupils.

"Were you able to rest a little, Grandma?" Evelyn asked affectionately.

Lea looked away, not knowing how to respond. The fact was that she had not been able to close her eyes in hours. Thousands of images had crossed her mind, never letting up. Tortuous memories returned to punish her, time after time, showing no mercy.

She nodded to her granddaughter's inquiry, avoiding any explanations on a subject that had already exhausted her and that she wasn't ready to take on with her granddaughter just yet.

"We're here!" Evelyn chimed, happily, as she felt the landing gear touch the ground.

The airplane executed a few pirouettes on the tarmac and after a several minutes came to a halt before an airport gate.

"I'm so glad we're here!" Evelyn enthusiastically said, as she got ready to get off the plane, motivating Lea to do the same.

Airport formalities were dispatched with quickly and as soon as they left the customs area they went in search of the driver that Victor had arranged for them, based on recommendations from a colleague who traveled to Warsaw frequently.

"Miss Evelyn Rotlewicz?" a gentleman asked politely, in English, but with a strong Eastern-European accent.

"That's me," she responded, happy that the driver was there waiting for them and that he knew her language.

"My name is Grzegorz Sortzinsky but you can call me Greg, since my full name is a little hard to pronounce."

"It's a pleasure to meet you," Lea said, extending her hand to him.

"All mine," he answered with an air of gallantry, opening the door so that they could get into the car that was parked just outside the terminal.

Evelyn studied him at length and concluded that—as her father had said—Greg seemed like a decent person, in the European mode…tall with salt-and-pepper hair…and some curious gestures when he spoke.

Once he took the wheel, he addressed them in respectful tones, turning his head to look behind him.

"Would you like to make the most of the day and tour Warsaw or shall we head straight to Ivansk? It's fifty miles away."

Lea and Evelyn glanced at one another, anxiously, and nearly said in unison: "We want to go to Ivansk."

The car started right away and after crossing a couple of major roads, they headed toward a highway-marked *Krakow.*

For a part of the journey, the car's occupants remained entirely silent, but once they reached the road to the northeast Greg asked them if they'd like to hear some information on Ivansk.

"We'd love to," Evelyn replied, sinking back into the seat.

"The original name of the settlement was Umishov and for some unknown reason, the inhabitants decided to change it to Ivansk—or Iwaniska in Polish.

"With the arrival of new inhabitants in 1403 they managed to reach the required number of residents and received the right to consider themselves a town.

"During the sixteenth century, Ivansk was one of Poland's Calvinist centers and important religious figures met there on certain occasions.

"The main highway that connects Warsaw to Krakow passes through Opatow, on the outskirts of Ivansk and between the two towns there is a highway that's easy to access, which is what gave rise to an important area trading center, with three annual fairs that attracted numerous merchants. Most decided to conduct their business from Ivansk.

"By 1578 Ivansk was home to fifteen clergymen who served the local nobility, nineteen distillers and 44 artisans. The vast majority of those artisans specialized in working gold, silver and steel.

"This period of prosperity ended in 1656. It is supposed that a great deal of the town was destroyed in a Swedish invasion that began in 1655. Only fifty houses were left in habitable conditions.

"During the eighteenth century the town of Ivansk was rebuilt, to accommodate 158 houses; and by 1869 there were 167 homes."

"Everything you're telling us is so interesting," Lea declared, impressed. "But how is it that living in Warsaw you've come to know so much about Ivansk?"

"That's easy, dear lady," Greg answered good humoredly. "I am an historian by profession and by avocation. My work as a driver and tourist guide helps me with everyday expenses, but my true passion is the history of Poland."

"Do you know anything about the Jews coming to Ivansk?" Evelyn pressed.

"We have no documented information about when the Jews first settled in Ivansk," Greg replied earnestly. "Most likely they arrived in the eighteenth century."

"Why did they settle in Ivansk and not in Warsaw?" Lea asked, curious.

"In those days a nobleman named Zwirowski, or Seborovsky—I can't quite remember—lived there," he said embarrassedly. "He was the Lord of the town. And he was convinced that the Jews' influence would be quite positive for Ivansk's development, so to attract them he allowed them to buy property and build their own residences."

"Then what happened?" Evelyn inquired, intrigued.

Greg took a deep breath and went on.

"By the mid-nineteenth century the Jewish community was well established and the construction of a wooden synagogue met the community's spiritual needs. Many Jews from nearby towns came to settle in Ivansk and the entire community worshipped in the only synagogue that then stood, under the religious leadership of Rabbi Yitzhak David Shapiro (1899). The young attended a traditional Jewish studies center called a *cheder*.

"From 1907 to 1914, Rabbi Yaakov presided over the community in Ivansk and was succeeded by Rabbi Yechiel Alter Ferleger. In 1924, Rabbi Yaakov Yitzchak Widman occupied the rabbinical chair until the outbreak of the Second World War."

"Wow!" Evelyn exclaimed. "I find it hard to believe you know so much about Ivansk, all the way down to the exact names, dates and events."|

Greg smiled. "Well as soon as your father's friend contacted me about this job, I decided to read up on Ivansk as much as I could, since I knew that Ivansk was going to be at the center of the trip."

"Thank you, Greg," Lea added, pleased. "It's marvelous to find people in life who are proud, and who enjoy not only doing their own work, but also helping others."

"I'm very pleased by what you have to say," said Greg, blushing. "But I have to tell you the truth.... Every time I have a client and he tells me in advance where he's going and what he has on his mind, I try to lay hands on as much historical material as possible so that the trip can be special, pleasant and informative. We're nearly to Opatow now," added Greg, making note of the sign by the side of the road. "Ivansk is not far off and we'll be there soon."

"Too bad we can't go on with the story, and just when Greg was starting to mention World War Two," Evelyn lamented with a deep sigh.

"We'll be there soon, sweetheart," Lea told her, thinking that the sigh was just sheer exhaustion.

Evelyn nodded and narrowed her eyes to lose herself in her own thoughts.

Chapter 16

It was the evening of that particular April day in spring, when they finally reached their destination.

The first impressions they had of Ivansk were of gentle hills and deep, dark forests that surrounded it, clean but deserted cobblestone streets, where time seemed to stand still. In contrast looking toward the countryside, the women could appreciate numerous herdsmen who drove donkeys and horses, which helped them with their duties to well-known destinations.

Greg stopped the car in front of a one-story wooden residence painted a shade of olive green, surrounded by tall trees, medium-sized shrubs and abundant moss.

"This is the house I was able to rent for you, for a few days," Greg said, satisfied, as he got out of the car to open the doors for them. "The owners are having financial difficulties," he added in a tentative tone, "and they decided to move out for as long as you need it. In the meantime they moved in with some close relatives."

Evelyn got out of the car immediately, with a curious gaze that seemed to want to take in everything. In the meantime Lea stepped out slowly, as the travel and previous night's lack of sleep had taken their toll on her; she felt exhausted.

"If you please, go inside while I unload the luggage," Greg invited solicitously. "I'll be with you in just a few minutes."

Evelyn crossed the threshold and marveled at the inside of the house, which in spite of being small was quite cozy.

The walls and ceilings were covered in horizontally cut tree trunks that had been artistically aligned. Solid dark wood furniture in the living and dining rooms spoke of good taste; a whitewashed kitchen, despite its reduced size, was immaculate and adorable, with white lace curtains and lots of homey details.

They went on to inspect the bedrooms and found that the wing to the right was split into two chambers: one, medium-sized, that featured a double bed and which they surmised was the master bedroom. The other bedroom, smaller, contained a simple bed and was adorned in pastel shades. "Surely it belonged to the daughter of the family," thought Evelyn, impressed.

"I hope the place suits you," said Greg as he put the suitcases down.

"It's a beautiful little house," Lea replied right away. "I think we'll be quite comfortable here."

"I'm glad to hear it," Greg said, pleased. "The owners left you some food in the refrigerator so you can have dinner tonight as well as breakfast tomorrow morning. I'll be going now, but I wanted to know if you needed anything else tonight—and what plans you have for tomorrow."

Evelyn promptly answered. "We'd like for you to take half the day off, since today was such a long day. In the meantime, we'll walk around a little to get to know the town; but after lunch I hope we can count on you to be our interpreter."

"With pleasure," Greg responded with a slight bow of the head. "So we'll see each other again tomorrow afternoon. Have a pleasant evening."

"Thanks—and good night," the women said, in unison.

The following day, Lea wore a lightweight, multicolored cotton dress and Evelyn put on some white pants and a long-sleeved hazelnut blouse, with athletic shoes and a casual bag that matched her top. Both were ready to go out after enjoying a delicious breakfast. They felt rested, even a little euphoric, since they had been able to sleep a whole night uninterrupted.

The day was clear and beautiful. They crossed the street that led them to the town's main square and market, a space for buying and selling all kinds of merchandise.

Once there, they lingered over the market's stalls. What attracted their attention most were different handicrafts, and they bought a handful of souvenirs. They also saw fruits, vegetables, grains, and a number of dairy products, but for the moment they decided not to buy food. They pressed on, heading down the street facing them, where they saw an enormous structure that was the church, next to a pharmacy, City Hall and the fire station.

"What now?" Lea asked.

"Let's go to the church," offered Evelyn. "I've heard that the parish priest is always on top of what's happening in any town. Hopefully he speaks English and will see us."

"Well, let's go then," Lea responded with enthusiasm.

Evelyn opened the heavy wooden door and let her grandmother enter, following directly behind. The sanctuary was shrouded in shadows. They began walking about slowly, to get familiar with their surroundings, until, as they approached the altar, they heard a voice call out to them in Polish. They looked at one another, not knowing what to do, as the parish priest drew near and asked how he could help them.

"We don't speak Polish," Lea said, shaking her head.

"English?" the priest asked politely.

"Yes, we speak English," Evelyn responded with relief.

"Ladies, how may I help you?" he asked attentively.

"We are visiting Ivansk. This lady is my grandmother and her name is Lea. My name is Evelyn and we live in the United States." The priest looked at them with interest but said nothing. "We'd like to know if you were here in Ivansk during the Second World War, when the Nazis came to carry off the Jews," Evelyn asked anxiously.

"Yes, madam, I was here— this is the town where I was born and raised. But I was too young to understand the implications of what was going on. That said, what I saw back then left an indelible mark both on my character as well as my life."

"Could you tell us what happened?" Lea implored.

"Yes, I'd be happy to," he answered. "But please, come with me to the sacristy where you'll be more comfortable, and where I can offer you a cup of tea."

"My life in Ivansk was peaceful," he said easily as he took a seat on a divan. *"I lived with my maternal grandmother since my parents died in an accident when I was just a tiny boy of two."*

He paused briefly, and then went on. *My grandmother was named Bozena and I came to love her like a true mother, since from the time I was orphaned she was devoted to me completely. I was quite happy because from the time the sun came up, Grandmother Bozena would let me go off with my friends and hang around the town from one end to another, singing and playing everywhere, with anything we used to find on the way. Ladies, I can truly say that was the most beautiful time I ever lived.*

But then one day everything changed. We had heard rumors that men belonging to a group called the Nazis had reached the neighboring towns, but we didn't pay too much attention until they came and installed themselves here.

At first nothing happened, but the soldiers impressed us with their haughty manner, their perfect uniforms, high, polished boots and strong German accents. Their air was calm, and sometimes they'd even greet us with an approving gesture or a wave.

On October 15th 1942, the day dawned cloudy. My grandmother worriedly told me not to stray too far from the house.

"Young man," she said, "remember that you're only nine, and ever since those Nazis showed up with their cars and their motorcycles, I haven't felt quite right unless I knew where you were, so please, be sure to check in with me often."

I was curious about Grandmother Bozena's attitude. It was the first time she had restricted my freedom to run around the town as I pleased. I decided I'd better obey. The future would prove her right.

It was still early in the morning that day. Several of my friends and I were sitting in the street in front of my house, playing marbles, when we suddenly heard some harsh shouts in German.

"Schnell, schnell—*get moving*—schnell."

We turned to see where those horrifying cries were coming from. Imagine our surprise when we saw these Nazis, ferocious expressions on their faces, carrying revolvers in their hands and aiming at people that had been our neighbors for years. We didn't understand what was happening but we began to cry and ran as quickly as we could to take refuge in our houses.

"Grandmother, Grandmother, where are you?" I cried out.

"What is it, Eugenio? Why are you shouting so?"

"They're taking our neighbors away, by force," I answered, anguished, as I clung to her.

"Calm down, little one," she responded as she stroked my head. "I want you to lie down for a bit while I go out to see what's happening."

"No grandmother! Don't leave me alone. I'm scared."

"I won't be long," she answered as she tried to comfort me. "I'm just going to stick my head out the door and then I'll come back."

I nodded, dubiously, but I let her go. When she returned an expression of horror covered her face. She could barely speak. "What's wrong with you, Grandmother Bozena?" I asked her fearfully. "What's happening?" She sat down on my bed slowly, with a far-off expression, as if she'd seen a ghost. She hugged me and said with anguish:

"They are carrying off our neighbors and a great many others besides."

"But why, Grandmother? What have they done wrong?"

"They didn't do anything wrong, sweetheart," she hastened to answer. "The problem is they are Jews."

"What does it matter if they're Jews?" I fired back. "I have lots of good Jewish friends, and their parents—and their brothers and sisters—are good too. So why are they taking them away if they haven't done anything bad?"

"Sweetheart, I don't know. Sometimes people with too much power play at being God, and manipulate other human beings to do what they want," my grandmother

answered worriedly.

The violent scenes repeated themselves, day after day, until one morning at dawn we heard a booming voice over a loudspeaker in the main square that announced, "All Jews of this town are to appear immediately in the main square. You may take one small suitcase only, containing your personal effects."

I saw several tears fall down my Grandmother Bozena's cheeks and I began to cry as well, because they were hauling off several of my best friends. I'd never treated them any different and I didn't care what their religion was—what mattered was how they treated me, the noble attitude they had, how extremely smart they were, the dedication they put into everything they set out to do and the wonderful families that surrounded them.

A few hours later I managed to escape from the house, even though Grandmother Bozena had forbidden me to go out, for fear the Nazis would think I was a Jew and hurt me. I stationed myself at the edge of the square, careful not to get too close, but close enough to see everything that was going on and I was shocked to see how many people were gathered there. Most were women who cried as they embraced their children, unable to understand what was happening, while the men, wanting to defend their families, clutched their fists in frustration. They'd witnessed how the Nazis murdered several people who tried to resist. Shots were heard repeatedly and several people fell to the ground, lifeless.

"I'd better get out of here," I said aloud when I saw what was happening. "They might grab me thinking I'm a

Jew."

That was the last time I saw my friends and their families. Years later I was able to find out what happened. First they were taken to the Warsaw Ghetto and then to the death camps.

Evelyn burst into inconsolable tears. The priest looked at her, frightened, thinking he had said something he shouldn't as Lea went to console her.

"Have I said something wrong?" the priest asked in confusion. "I thought you wanted to know what happened in Ivansk in the Second World War."

"Forgive me, Father, I couldn't help reacting that way," said Evelyn, drying her tears. She then began to relate to the priest the reason why she and Lea had decided to make such a long, but important journey. When she finished her story, the priest was left staring at her.

"Do you think you'll be able to discover something that belongs to a past life?" he asked incredulously.

"Yes, Father, I do. My happiness—my life—depends on it."

"May God help you in your search. And if there is anything else I can do to help you, do not hesitate to ask," he offered as he rose from the divan to say goodbye.

"Thank you so much, Father," said Lea as she took her leave. "You don't know how important your story has been to us."

"I am happy for that, my daughters, and I hope you'll come back to see me before leaving Ivansk."

"It will be a pleasure, Father. We'll be sure to do

that," Evelyn added with conviction.

Chapter 17

Walking across the town square, in utter silence, served to help them clear their heads.

"How can something so horrible and inhuman have happened in this town?" wondered Evelyn, as an anguished Lea stared silently ahead.

After ten minutes they reached the house, and as soon as they went in Evelyn noticed the strange expression that washed over Lea's face.

"Grandma, are you all right?" she asked with concern.

"Yes, sweetheart, I'm okay—but I need to speak with you."

"We'll talk in a minute. Relax while I go to the bathroom," Evelyn asked as she helped her settle into the living room sofa.

Just then there was a knock at the door and Lea got up to answer it with an absent air.

"Good afternoon, *Madame*," Greg greeted her amiably.

"Please come in," she requested, and then returned to the sofa.

"Your granddaughter—she isn't here?"

"She'll be right out...please, sit down."

"Thank you," he replied as he took her up on the offer.

"I'm happy you're here," Evelyn said as she entered the room a few minutes later, with an affable smile.

"Thank you, Miss," he quickly replied with a respectful rise as Evelyn settled in next to Lea.

"Have a seat, Greg, and please go on with the story you were telling us on the way to Ivansk, the story that had to do with when the Nazis reached town."

"Of course...with pleasure," he answered, taking a seat in an armchair that was near the sofa where the women were seated. "*A small contingent of Germans entered Ivansk on September 7th, 1939*," said Greg in consultation with a small notebook he pulled from his shirt pocket. He paused, then went on...

At first there were no problems since the Germans didn't interfere with the daily routine, because they didn't know the area well and Polish officials or police were handling any incidents that might have taken place. But the situation changed in mid-1941 when the Germans started demanding "maintenance" money from the Polish government; the government extracted the money from its citizens. As the Germans' demands became more extreme, the Polish government began asking for more money from Jewish groups, with no hesitation about the fact that they had to pay for other people in the town.

The Germans enacted oppressive anti-Jewish laws that affected Ivansk and all of occupied Poland.

Greg cleared his throat and went on. *All Jews were forced to wear yellow armbands with the Star of David so they could always be identified, preventing them from having a normal life with the rest of the population, especially when it came to the ban on doing business with non-Jews.*

This unleashed a tragic economic chaos that ultimately kept them from acquiring basic food needed to stay alive. Hunger, disease and desperation created unsustainable situations.

A young rabbi named Rabinovitz, very active among the Jews, a Zionist and opposed to the ultra-orthodox Hasidim, created a special service to help those most in need of food, including Jews from Vienna whom the war had driven to Ivansk as refugees and who found themselves in deplorable circumstances.

Toward the end of 1941, members of a German construction company called the Todt Organization came to Ivansk with the idea of deporting young, healthy Jews to forced-labor camps where survival was all but impossible. Faced with such a prospect, Rabbi Rabinovitz and other members of that early Zionist youth group encouraged the young men to flee into the forest rather than suffer deportation.

They created an underground movement in 1942, in Ivansk, started stockpiling food, purchased weapons and made plans to escape in small groups, to nearby woods where they had outfitted hiding places, despite the fact that the Hasidim opposed organizing underground cells, arguing it was better to do what the Germans ordered, since only a miracle—"divine intervention"—could save them.

In May 1942, the Nazis started deporting Jews to concentration camps from the towns surrounding Ivansk. In autumn 1942, Jewish leaders in Ivansk learned the exact date the Nazis planned to ship them out.

Rabbi Rabinovitz asked his followers and the Zionist pioneers to help him bury the Torah, the prayer books and other sacred objects in the Jewish cemetery. The day before the deportation, 1600 Jews attended the burial and in a solemn ceremony, Rabbi Rabinovitz made a farewell address, asking God's help in the new life they would have to face, and he urged all present to try to save their own lives and the lives of their loved ones.

Some three hundred Jews—men, women and children—fled Ivansk to seek refuge in the woods, led by Rabbi Rabinovitz. On October 15th 1942, the Gestapo and members of the Ukrainian police surrounded the town and forced Jews out of their houses and into the main square.

The Nazis searched every residence, every corner of the town, killing anyone who tried to hide in defiance of their orders. The Jews of Ivansk were first taken to the ghetto at Cmielow, under strict surveillance, and from there to Ostrowice and then on to Warsaw, where they were loaded onto boxcars and transported to the concentration camp at Auschwitz to be exterminated. Only one Jew from Ivansk, named Israel Seltzer, managed to escape Auschwitz and recounted the murderous story to others of his faith.

The Gestapo hunted down and captured the three hundred Jews who fled to the forests surrounding Ivansk. With the help of the Poles who knew the terrain, and police dogs, they were shot on sight, without mercy.

Greg paused and made as if he might go on, when he saw Lea's face awash in tears. He decided it was better to stop.

"Thank you, Greg, for teaching us so much about Ivansk," Evelyn said as she dried tears of her own. "Without your help we wouldn't have been able to finish what we needed to do here so quickly. I think, in fact, there's no more for us to do here, and if my Grandma is in agreement we'll continue on our journey after saying goodbye to the priest who also helped us a great deal on this search."

"As you wish," Greg answered anxiously.

After a short talk between Lea and Evelyn, they decided to give Greg the rest of the day off, so that they could start out early from Ivansk once they said goodbye to the priest.

"I'll see you tomorrow, then," he said politely as he left.

"See you tomorrow," they answered.

Lea walked slowly to the living room sofa; meanwhile Evelyn closed the door as Greg left.

"Evelyn, could you sit down here for a minute? I want to talk to you," Lea asked as she heard her granddaughter draw near.

"Of course, Grandma," she answered tenderly, as she sat down next to her.

"What I'm about to tell you is a secret that I've kept for many years and I've only shared with Abraham, who has told no one, in deference to my wishes." She paused, briefly, and then went on.

My parents were good, hard-working people that managed to give me a happy childhood, where I felt protected, and even indulged, despite the fact we weren't from an upper class background. I never lacked for the essentials and they gave me the tools I needed to take on life.

When I turned fifteen I was introduced to a Polish man named Elias Wolovisky as well as to his parents. They told me that soon he would be my husband.

As soon as those people left my house I begged my parents in tears not to marry me off to him, because in addition to being much older than I, he had left such a bad impression on me that it even made me shudder.

"I'm sorry, Lea," my father replied. "But we've already given our word that you are to become his wife and we shook hands on it. In Judaism that's an iron-clad contract."

I kept on crying and begged them daily not to make me get married, reminding them of how young I was and the dreams I still had, but it was all in vain. Three months later, in front of the rabbi, I was married to Elias.

My life as a married woman became an ordeal. His tastes differed from mine in every way, but the worst was that he loved to drink and no day passed that he didn't get drunk.

My two boys Joel and Michael were born from that rocky union and they became the center of my life, as well as of Elias's, who, despite his benders, never abused them, only me. Depending on how drunk he was, he would insult me or beat me savagely, from time to time. I ended up wishing for death at twenty years old since except looking out for my children, there was nothing I cared about and nothing made me happy.

I talked to my parents time and again, relating my sorrows and asking for their help, but they resisted believing me and I lived desperately, not knowing what to do. It was then that I thought about killing myself as the only way out.

But my boys! What would become of them, deprived of a mother and left with an alcoholic father?

"Dear God, help me bear this difficult, incomprehensible situation," I would beseech the Almighty, day and night, not knowing what to do.

One day, four years after marrying Elias, I met your grandfather.

Abraham worked as a traveling salesman and had been in a business relationship with my father for the previous six years. He was young…handsome…of medium height…and he had the sweetest eyes, eyes that looked at me differently. I believed I saw a great deal of tenderness in his glance.

What happened between us was nothing we planned. It happened one day like any other when my father took ill, which didn't occur often, and he asked me to fill in for him at his clothing store.

I sat down behind the counter, immersed in my own thoughts, trying to find some solution to my everyday life, and grew bored watching the hours pass without anyone coming into the store.

"What's wrong, Lea?" Abraham asked me as he entered the store and saw me in such an anguished state

"Nothing, nothing," I said, flustered and turning red with embarrassment.

"Forgive me if I startled you," he answered with concern when he saw my lips were trembling. And then something uncanny happened…when I heard Abraham speak to me affectionately I began to cry…and cry and cry, letting loose the feelings that had been inside of me.

Abraham drew me to his chest and began to stroke my hair and I let him go on, sobbing to let loose my bitterness. After quite some time I managed to calm down, begging him not to mention the scene he had just witnessed to anyone.

"I promise I won't tell anyone about what happened—if you'll tell me why there is so much pain bottled up inside you."

At first I doubted if I should let him in on my problems, since he was little more than a stranger to me. But I felt this huge weight that bore down on my heart and there was no one else I could share my troubles with.

So I decided to trust him and I began to tell him about the life my children and I were facing, ever since the day I'd become Elias's wife.

"Oh, you poor thing," he exclaimed tenderly when I had finished my story. "How can they treat you so harshly, when you're just a young, frightened girl who's only starting out in life? And what have your parents said about all this? Or have you not told them how that bastard treats you?" Abraham asked, deeply impressed.

"I've told them everything," I answered, sobbing. "But they don't believe me and they don't want to get involved in my marital problems."

"They should be ashamed!" Abraham declared angrily. "It's not enough just to bring children into this world—you must protect them until the end of their days."

"Abraham, don't speak that way about them. I don't want anything bad to happen to them—I love them very much, they're good people—but it's terrible that they are so dogmatic."

"But that doesn't give them the right to damage someone's life, much less their own daughter's, submitting her to a miserable existence!" he shouted furiously.

"Abraham, calm down," I asked tenderly. "Even though my current situation leaves me desperate, I still believe there is a God who sees all and that somehow is going to help me."

"You are right," he answered more calmly.

Time passed and our relationship grew stronger each time we met. I had a hand in making that happen, offering to fill in for my dad at the store perhaps too frequently.

I remember vividly one special afternoon when

Abraham came in quite excited. I'd never seen him that way and as he hugged me he said, "Lea, I have just been offered a job in the United States, in Florida. I've been waiting for this chance for years and finally today I got a letter that conveyed the good news. A close friend of my parents went there a few years back to make a better life for himself and once he got established he sent for his family and now, my darling Lea, he remembered me. He always said I was a great salesman and that one day he was going to offer me a job. Now he's opened a fabric business, and since things are going well he wants me there beside him."

"So you are planning on going to Florida?" I asked anxiously.

"You'd better believe it," he answered, elated. "This is a once-in-a-lifetime opportunity and I'm not going to let it get away."

"So that means I'm never going to see you again?" I asked, upset.

"You don't want to come with me?" he asked right away.

"What are you saying, Abraham? I am a married woman—with two children. I care nothing about my husband, but my children—how can I leave them to their fate when they are still so young?"

"Let's take them with us," he answered rapidly.

"Elias will follow us to the ends of the earth to get his children back, I know that much about him," I insisted, "and he's a man so full of anger that after he found us, he would be capable of killing us in vengeance."

"Darling, let's run away and begin a new life in the United States. Look, you have been tempted to kill yourself several times—do you think that's fair to you?"

"How can I abandon my children?" I asked, exhausted.

"We will have other children," he answered serenely. "And besides, you have always told me that Elias treats the children very well. Why is he going to change now?"

"I don't know...I don't know..." I muttered with fright. "I need time to think about this—I am all turned around right now."

"Lea, do you love me?" he asked solemnly.

"With all my heart, darling," I answered, so sure that it made me shudder just to think of it.

"Then why all these doubts?" he asked, drawing near. He took me in his arms and kissed me with such passion that at that very moment I decided my future and my happiness were by his side and nothing else in life mattered.

"Oh, Grandma...my beloved grandma, you don't know what an effect your story has had on me. I'm sorry for what you have been through in life," Evelyn said, tears in her eyes, as she stood up from the sofa to embrace her. "I don't know what I would have done in your shoes, since I don't have children and can't know the magnitude of what it means to be a mother...but just thinking about a life condemned to suffering breaks my heart."

Lea pulled out of her granddaughter's embrace, and when she sat back down on the sofa, acknowledged:

"Despite the amazing life I've had at your grandfather's side, I don't think that if I had it to do over again I'd make the mistake of leaving my boys...you cannot know the nostalgia, the loneliness, the hell that I have lived all these years, wondering how they are, how they were treated, what chance they ever had or if they ever were able to forgive me for abandoning them."

"Grandma, we'll find them," Evelyn assured her cautiously.

"If we only could," Lea sighed. "I need for them to forgive me and to understand the circumstances that led me to leave them behind back then. I want to see them...know they are all right and to tell them how much I missed them and how much I love them."

Chapter 18

The following day dawned somewhat rainy, but it didn't keep Greg from putting the luggage into the trunk of the car and helping Lea and Evelyn get in. Once he was certain they were comfortably settled, he took the wheel, released the brake and the journey was underway.

Most of the trip took place in silence, which struck Greg as strange after the previous journey's experience with these women had been one of amenable conversation and unending interest in what had happened in his country. He had enjoyed being able to share his knowledge with them.

Lea was nodding in and out when they reached the hotel and Evelyn, looking on affectionately, did not want to wake her.

"Grandma, wake up—we're here."

"Oh! I fell asleep," Lea replied, slowly pulling herself together as she fixed her hair.

When they got out of the car they saw that Greg had already taken the suitcases out of the trunk and placed them on the hotel bellman's cart. They went in to the front desk and once they had registered, went up to the room they had been assigned at the same time that Greg placed the bags on their respective stands.

"Thank you so much for your help, Greg," Evelyn said to him. "Our trip wouldn't be the same without you. Now please feel free to go to your room and rest a while. We're going to do the same and we'll be ready to go out after lunch."

"Is there somewhere in particular you wish to go?" Greg asked.

"Grandma and I decided to go to different places, as a better way of getting what we came for," Evelyn answered quickly. "I have an interview today that the priest in Ivansk arranged for me, at the home of a man named Mr. Seltzer, and I'd like for you to take me there. In the meantime, if you could please take grandma to city hall and accompany her while she does what she needs to do; then pick me up at the same address where you dropped me off.

"Of course, with pleasure," Greg answered. He picked up his bag and took his leave.

After lunch they all met at the hotel main entrance.

Once back in the car, Greg yet again remarked how quiet the women were but didn't know to what to attribute the change.

When they reached the first destination, Evelyn verified the address was the same as the one she had jotted down in a notebook.

"Take care Grandma" she said, kissing Lea on the cheek. Encouraging Greg to look after her grandmother, she stepped down from the car.

When she approached the door of the house, which was ajar, she saw an older man saying goodbye to a still-quite-beautiful old woman. She saw them hug tightly.

"I'll write often," she heard the woman say to him.

"You cannot know how much I'm going to miss you," he answered with regret, escorting her to the exit where a driver awaited in an SUV. He helped her get into the vehicle, they said goodbye one last time and when he turned to go back to the house he caught sight of Evelyn.

"How may I help you, Miss?" he asked quizzically.

"I'm looking for Mr. Israel Seltzer."

"I am Israel Seltzer," he said, raising an eyebrow.

"The priest at Ivansk told me he had requested you receive me. I am Evelyn Rotlewicz and I have come from the United States."

"Oh, of course I remember the reverend father's call," he answered abashedly. "Please come into my house. I grew so sentimental at my sister's parting—she is moving to France—that I think it left me a little foolish."

Evelyn scanned the old house, furnished and decorated with pieces from the 1950s, and following their owner's indications she took a seat.

"May I offer you anything to drink?" he asked courteously.

"No, thank you," she responded. "I just had lunch."

The two looked at each other for just a moment and

then Evelyn began to speak. "The priest at Ivansk told me you were one of the few people who managed to escape from the concentration camp at Auschwitz. By any chance did you ever have an opportunity to meet a man by the name of Duvid Zonchtein?"

"My dear young woman, so many years have gone by since everything happened that I have forgotten a lot. But that name in particular I could never get out of my mind," he said with decision.

Evelyn shivered at the acknowledgement and continued to listen.

I remember that dreadful night when suddenly the barrack door number 37 at Auschwitz, where I and some thirty other men lived, opened. A sinister looking, solidly built Nazi shoved Duvid to force him to enter, causing him to roll on the floor as the guard barked, "Schnell, schnell"—*"hurry up, hurry up..."*

Minutes later he clicked his heels drily; turned and hurriedly left the building. I looked over at the new arrival and I was able to make out the disbelief and pallor that spread across his face.

"Please, get up and sit on the bunk," one of my barrack-mates suggested, seeing him so utterly confused.

Duvid did what had been suggested and I took the opportunity to go over to him and sit by his side.

"I don't understand what has happened," the newcomer worriedly declared.

"What do you mean?" I answered in a low voice.

"My wife and I got off the train and as soon as we arrived all these soldiers began to push us and shout at us

in German. They stripped us of our belongings and separated us, sending me to the line with the men, my wife toward the women's line. After a long wait, I ended up in front of this German's desk. He interrogated me in words I could not understand then ordered me to move on to the right. Then, by pure coincidence, I saw how they were leading off my wife in the opposite direction from me. I tried to run over to where she was, but the soldiers kept me from doing it, beating me so fiercely that I nearly passed out. Then they brought me here."

I lowered my gaze to keep Duvid from seeing the tears that had started to fall from my eyes, since I'd been through something similar not many days previously and I still wasn't able to understand the reasons behind all this horror and cruelty.

"Where is my wife? What have they done with her?" he asked in a frenzy.

A barracks-mate who had been living in the concentration camp for months, came over to Duvid and exclaimed, "Just forget about her!"

"But what are you saying—are you out of your mind?" he replied angrily.

"Since you got here, haven't you noticed a stench of burnt flesh?"

Duvid nodded yes.

"Those are the ovens in the crematorium, incinerating human beings. I would not be surprised if that's where they took your wife."

"What this man is saying cannot be true," Duvid shouted in desperation.

"It is," the man answered bitterly. And at that moment the thirty men began to recite The Prayer for the Dead.

"Yis-gad-dal v'yis-kad-dash sh'mey rab-bo..."

Days went by and Duvid, hanging his head, could not stop thinking and talking about his wife and their two children. The thought he could not defend his wife as the Nazis were leading her off tormented him and he felt guilty for having let his children get off the truck. I always told him that maybe because of the decision they'd made then, the children might have some chance of saving their own lives.

He always answered with an affirmative gesture, but with an infinite expression of sorrow. The work we were assigned daily was exhausting. We didn't have the right clothes for such a bitter winter and our shoes—that barely even had soles—chafed our feet.

"Let's run away from here, Duvid," I would plead with him each day, but he would look back in doubt, thinking that there could be a miracle and that he would see his wife and children again. I, on the other hand, knew with certainty that my wife had died. Nothing in that place held me back.

One night several Nazis came to Barrack number 37 to report to us that a prisoner had gone missing and that the punishment to rectify such disorder—as they would have it—was to hang several of the men who lived in the barrack. The following morning they chose them at random and one of them was Duvid.

That devastating event led to my decision to run

away, which I had the chance to do four days later when we went out to work on a highway and the Nazi in charge of watching us grew distracted talking about his girlfriend to another guard.

I slipped away as best I could and then started running and running without following any fixed path, until I got as far away as I could. Then I decided to walk next to the train tracks, which were like a guide, and wherever I went, I tried to scrounge up something to eat, even if it meant stealing.

It took a great deal of time to reach Warsaw. I didn't want to go back to Ivansk because I was aware that the people I once knew were no longer living there; that most had been murdered in the ovens at Auschwitz.

As soon as I got to Warsaw I began to tell people what I had been through, above all everything I knew about the cremation ovens. No one believed me—they thought I was a madman.

"How could I ask for help with something so tragic, so inhumane and so unbelievable?" Mr. Seltzer said to Evelyn as he hid his face in his hands.

"Forgive me for making you relive so much agony; it wasn't my intention," Evelyn begged him with remorse.

"Please, don't worry," Mr. Seltzer responded more calmly. "It's just that in addition to the terrible experience I went through…they killed my entire family except for the sister you saw when you arrived, because she was out of the country when the Nazis arrived, as well as the 1600 people they shipped out of Ivansk, most of whom were my neighbors and friends, as often happens in small towns."

"I understand so much now, especially why the priest in Ivansk insisted I come see you. When we said goodbye, he explained to me that you had been the only survivor from the men and women that they transported from Ivansk to the Auschwitz death camp. I'd like, if I may, to tell you my story, which is the reason behind why I asked to speak with you."

Evelyn began to tell him her story, starting when she was five: the nightmares, the anguish, and the desperation of not knowing what had happened to her husband and children in a past life; the insecurity she felt about marrying a man whom she loved, yet knowing that she was going to drag him into that unrelenting crossroads of yesterday.

"My God, what an astounding story! Let me tell you, Evelyn, if I may call you that, I am a believer in past lives, since I heard such fantastic stories back in the concentration camp, but yours goes beyond any I ever heard before, above all when I see that you are a person who really has experienced that entire cycle of nightmares and horrifying daydreams."

"Thank you for everything, Mr. Seltzer. It means a lot to me to know what happened to Duvid, despite how tragic his death was. It's really tough not knowing what happened to the people that made up such an important family group in one's life."

"Of course it is," he answered pensively. And I want to let you know that Bluma also died in the concentration camp and Duvid found that out before he died on the gallows. One day they sent him to the dispensary because he had cut and infected his foot in a number of places and as luck would have it, the nurse that saw him was originally from Ivansk. She related that Bluma had fallen ill from typhus, which meant they took her straight to the ovens."

Israel Seltzer paused and then went on...

"From that moment on, Duvid lost any will to live, even though deep down he felt his children were still alive."

"And that's my next task—finding Duvid and Bluma's children," Evelyn explained nervously.

At that very instant Israel Seltzer's doorbell rang and he got up to answer it.

"Evelyn, there's a man here who's looking for you."

"Please ask him to wait outside for just a minute," she requested.

Israel Seltzer returned to where Evelyn was and in a burst of emotion she hugged him tightly. They stayed there for a while until she, separating from him, exclaimed, "Oh, thank you, thank you...thank you so much, Mr. Seltzer. If it weren't for you I would never have found out what happened to Duvid and Bluma."

"I'm happy to have been able to help you with your search, my dear. And now a new day awaits you that is as important as the one that came before it."

"It's true," she stated. "And I'm going to take it on with a whole new spirit."

"There you go! And may luck be with you!"

Chapter 19

Evelyn got into the car and drew near to Lea to give her a kiss on the cheek.

"How did it go, Grandma? Were you able to find anything out?" she asked with interest.

Lea looked back with infinite sadness.

"No, Evelyn, I wasn't able to get my hands on anything. All I managed to find out was that on the 22nd of January 1933, Hitler and the Nazis took control of Germany and took up a campaign against the Jews as they began preparations to conquer all of Europe. In a time of such instability, Elias decided to leave the country and carried my children off with him, leaving nary a trace. Maybe he did it to protect himself or to punish me, thinking that one day I was going to come looking for them again. He wanted to make sure we weren't reunited.

"To think that their own mother cannot see them before she dies!" she exclaimed desperately as she burst into tears.

Greg saw them through the rearview mirror without knowing what was happening. He watched as tears fell down Evelyn's beautiful face while she tried to console Lea, unsuccessfully. Then he released the brake and, saying nothing, headed the car toward the hotel.

Once they reached their room, Evelyn gave Lea a tranquilizer and helped her undress, staying by her side for a while as the older woman slept. Then she got on the phone to the United States.

"Hello? Hello? Who's speaking please?" Victor asked.

"Daddy, it's me!" exclaimed Evelyn excitedly. "How are you, Mom and Grandpa Abraham?"

"We're all fine, sweetheart. How's the trip going for you and your grandmother?"

"It's going well, Dad," she replied. "Grandma was exhausted and is lying down for a while. We've delved into quite a bit of research and today I feel better after having been able to discover what happened to Duvid and Bluma, even though they were killed at Auschwitz. But, I still need to find out what happened to their children Ariel and Ethel."

"So what are you going to do?" he asked, curious.

"I'm thinking that if it's all right with you and mom, I'm going to go to France. I don't know if you remember in one of the hypnosis sessions with Dr. Eidelman, when Tamara Ianofsky, Bluma's friend, told her that they had taken the children to France, to "Maison Izieu," a summer camp for children, and that they would be safe there."

"Yes, I do remember that, honey, but I wonder if that place even exists anymore or if anyone can tell you anything about it."

"Dad, I've got to give it a shot."

"I know. So keep going."

"Thanks for understanding, Dad, and for your support. Send my regards to Mom—she must be playing cards with her friends about now—and to Grandpa Abraham, too. I'm going to call him right after this."

"Take care of yourself, Evelyn. When are you thinking of leaving for France?"

"I haven't decided yet but it's got to be soon. I'm really anxious to be back home with you."

"We miss you a lot, too, honey."

"We'll talk soon, Dad," she said a little sadly.

"Until then, sweetheart."

She kept the receiver in her hands for a few seconds more and then purposefully dialed the US again.

"Hello, who's calling?" she heard the person who answered say.

"Grandpa, it's me, Evelyn."

"How are you, my darling little girl? And how's that wife of mine?"

"We're good, Grandpa. Grandma is resting and I wanted to take the opportunity to tell you that she let me in on the secret you both have kept for so many years. She's been looking into the whereabouts of her two children but unfortunately this person Elias left the country in 1933 and took the children with him."

"Oh, my, that's not good," he responded in consternation.

"It hasn't been a good day for her, Grandpa. I don't know what to do. Now I'm thinking of going to France to continue my investigation. But after Grandma realized she wasn't going to be able to see her children it's really gotten her down and I'm not sure if she'll want to press on with me or return to the States."

"Well, ask her," he advised.

"That's what I'll do, Grandpa. We'll talk soon."

"Send Lea a big hug, and tell her I'll be anxiously awaiting her call."

Lea went in and out of sleep, or deeply buried in her thoughts, for several days, evincing no interest in food. As she tried to comfort her grandmother, Evelyn found it hard to face such a painful situation, especially when it involved someone she loved, so much, suffering in such a way.

One day Evelyn got up her courage and, going into Lea's room, declared, "Grandma, I've got to talk to you,"

Lea nodded her assent.

"We've gone several days without moving ahead on our work, and for me to go on, I need to go to France, which was the last place mentioned in one of the hypnosis sessions I had with Dr. Eidelman about where Bluma's children ended up. I want to know if you'd like to come with me to France or if you'd rather return to the States."

Lea delayed before responding. "I'll go with you to France," she replied, her mind made up. "I couldn't leave you on your own."

"Thank you, Grandma," she said, embracing her, at the same time feeling relief that she could pull her out of the depression she'd fallen into. "So I'll get started on the preparations for the trip."

Lea nodded once more.

The next day began with a great deal of activity: leaving the hotel, the trip to the airport, checking in and checking bags. The toughest part was saying goodbye to their faithful companion Greg.

"Thank you so much, Greg," Evelyn said, embracing him. "Without you our trip would have been so difficult. Your help and dedication have been invaluable. It's what allowed us to finish what we came for and for that we'll always be thankful. I hope this is not a goodbye, but rather a see-you-soon. We hope to meet again someday."

Greg looked at them thankfully, and smiled as he said, "It's been a real pleasure to have been there for you, and I'm especially pleased you found some solutions to your problems."

Lea extended her hand as she said: "Thank you for everything." He took her hand and kissed it.

"Goodbye, my dear lady. Something inside tells me that you're going to see your children again. It's just a matter of time."

"Thanks again and so long—for now," Lea answered sadly.

Chapter 20

"MAISON IZIEU". Evelyn read the sign by the entrance and her heart shuddered at the thought of discovering what had become of Ariel and Ethel.

She rang the bell, and as she waited for someone to open the door, she felt a knot in her stomach. She thought it was due to not having time to stop anywhere to eat since leaving Lyon.

"How may I help you, *mademoiselle*?" an older woman asked in French.

"Do you speak English?" Evelyn inquired hesitantly.

"Of course," the woman responded in a perfect accent.

"Forgive me for bothering you, *Madame*, I know these are not standard visiting hours, but I'm very anxious to speak with someone who knows the history of this place and the children who once lived here."

"Follow me, please," the woman responded cordially. "I am Margot Pasteur, and I have run the house for years. I'm delighted to meet those who have a genuine interest in discovering the true story of what happened to its inhabitants. May I offer you some tea, perhaps some biscuits?"

"I'd be quite grateful," Evelyn answered, once again hearing her stomach rumble from hunger.

They settled into the small parlor where Madame Pasteur had led them, and after taking a sip of a wonderful English tea and cookies served with it, Evelyn felt comfortable taking up the matter that had brought her there.

"Madame Pasteur," she said warmly, "you are an incredible hostess. Would it bother you too much if I asked you a few questions?"

"On the contrary, I'd be delighted if I could help."

"Could you tell me a little bit about Maison Izieu?" Evelyn asked nervously.

"Of course," she answered as she began to tell her story.

Between 1940 and 1941 the French people were exhausted and demoralized by the nation's fall and concerned about socioeconomic problems it faced. The nation did not react, as it should, with regard to the Nazi persecution of the Jews.

The sole entity that acted in the face of this brazen anti-Semitism was a charitable organization known as "Oeuvre de Secours aux Enfants"—the OSE—created in Russia in 1912 to support Jewish and non-Jewish young people's potential social and medical needs.

Starting in 1941, many children were housed at an

OSE House in Palavas-les-Flots, where organization members liberated them from Vichy boarding schools, attended to their needs in general and sought to protect them from deportation to death camps. This was part of an initiative of a couple, two charitable individuals named Miron Zlatin—who was a distinguished agronomist—and Sabine Zlatin, a nurse with the French Red Cross. They also enjoyed support from the prefect of the Department of Hérault, a man by the name of Bénédetti.

When the Department of Hérault began to fall apart at the beginning of 1943, yet another consequence of the war, the prefect suggested that the Zlatins relocate to the small village of Izieu, not far from Lyon, since the area was controlled by Italian, rather than French forces.

A few weeks later, Miron and Sabine Zlatin and 44 children ages three to thirteen, along with seven instructors, moved to Maison Izieu, unoccupied during most of the year and only used by a Catholic school during summer vacation. There they regrouped and began to live their everyday lives. But the Italian capitulation, in September 1943, brought on Nazi occupation and in February 1944, the Gestapo arrested a number of OSE collaborators, which led to the organization's decision to close all its children's shelters at once.

On April 6, 1944, under the leadership of Klaus Barbie, the notorious "butcher of Lyon," the Gestapo stormed the house and arrested the children and their teachers with the exception of a medical student named Leon Reifman, who managed to escape through a window, and Sabine Zlatin, who wasn't at home at the time.

Forty-two children and five adults were sent via various transports from Drancy to Auschwitz-Birkenau, where they were murdered.

The only survivor from that group was a teacher, Lea Feldblum, who was put to work at the camp as a means of separating her from the children she so loved. She recounted the events that occurred after the house was raided.

Two youths and the shelter director, Miron Zlatin, were deported to Estonia and were killed there in the summer of 1944. In 1987, in Lyon, added Madame Pasteur, with a pause, *Klaus Barbie was extradited from Bolivia and tried for crimes against humanity. He was then sentenced to life imprisonment. At the same time the trial was taking place, Sabine Zlatin started a new non-profit organization.*

On April 24, 1994 French President François Mitterrand paid tribute to the children and their teachers. That day La Maison Izieu, where they had lived, as well as an adjacent farm, were officially recognized and a museum was created to commemorate the history and events that had taken place there. I should also tell you about the fate of another eleven thousand Jewish children who were deported from France to be exterminated at various concentration camps.

"Oh, dear God," whispered Evelyn, trembling and holding back tears.

"Do you know how many grown men and women were deported from France, with cooperation on the part of the French police, to be annihilated in concentration camps?" Madame Pasteur asked Evelyn.

The latter shook her head in denial.

"All told, the Germans deported seventy-five thousand Jews from France. Most were transported on freight trains to Auschwitz."

Evelyn could take no more at that point and broke into desperate sobs.

"I'm sorry my story has frightened you," Madame Pasteur declared with regret. "But these are real events that kept me from sleeping when I first came to this house. Above all as I began to study each separate case, I saw photographs of the children, of their families and the papers that ordered their deportation to other countries. They were forcibly torn from their families and thrown into horrible facilities, whose conditions could only be partially mitigated through collaboration on the part of the adults that had been in charge of them at Maison Izieu."

"I'm so thankful to you for telling me the story of this place," said Evelyn as she dried her tears. "But now I hope I can ask you about two children I'm looking for, who I believe lived here at Maison Izieu."

Madame Pasteur stared back incredulously, and then asked, "Who are you talking about?"

"Ariel and Ethel Zonchtein."

"How do you know of those children?" Madame Pasteur all but shouted.

It was then that Evelyn began to tell her story to Madame Pasteur and when she finished she saw the older woman rise and approach, to embrace her as she said, "My poor young woman, how you have suffered. I'm going to look into the record books and see if I can help you. The surname you mention sounds familiar to me. Please give me just a moment."

Evelyn nodded and began to wait. Madame Pasteur came back in after a few minutes with a book in her hands.

"These are the records of the children that lived in this house," Madame Pasteur declared as she sat down. "Everything from their parents' names to who brought them here, when they left, and even if they were part of the Gestapo raid in which Klaus Barbie participated."

"Please look for the children's names," Evelyn requested nervously.

"Here they are," Madame Pasteur answered. She went on: "Ariel Zonchtein was born in Poland on April 15, 1934, the son of Duvid Zonchtein, born in Poland in 1908, and his wife Bluma Feldman Zonchtein, also born in Poland, in 1911. He was brought to Maison Izieu by a representative of the French consulate who stated that Morris and Tamara Ianofsky gave him the child, after he explained that the children's parents had been the victims of a Nazi roundup in Poland and that they had decided to send the boy to France, to prevent him from being deported to Auschwitz."

"Oh, dear God, dear God" shouted Evelyn, unable to contain herself. "I lived all of that in my nightmares—the names, the places, everything that happened. How is it possible that all of that occurred?"

Madame Pasteur stared back at her then said, "For

mystics, *déjà-vu* is nothing more than the logical consequence of reincarnation and psychologists also agree that these sensations bear some important message for those who perceive them. In this case you experienced a series of emotions and lived events, that, when analyzed, allowed you to understand the meaning of the pain you experienced in a previous life—as you shouldered its unbearable weight in your present existence, not knowing what had happened to your husband and children."

"And does Ethel also appear in your records?"

Madame Pasteur consulted the registry once more and found the name of Ethel Zonchtein, born in Poland on August 18, 1935, to the same parents as Ariel. The record stated she was Ariel's sister and that the same representative of the French Consulate who had brought her brother, delivered her to Maison Izieu, also on behalf of Morris and Tamara Ianofsky.

"Yes!" Evelyn exclaimed excitedly. "Finally I've found them. Thank you so much for your help, Madame Pasteur."

"Young friend, sit down, please," the older woman pleaded, almost in a whisper.

"Is something wrong?" Evelyn asked uneasily.

"I'm afraid so," Madame Pasteur answered with a pained expression.

The report says the OSE created a resistance network that implied illegal activity in order to hide and clothe the children. It also used professionals to forge identity papers and carried out clandestine movements, to take the children from France to non-aligned countries where their lives would be spared. They also made arrangements so that whatever happened that might cause the OSE to disappear, the work would continue.

To that end they drew up lists of the children's names in code, which they sent to Geneva, where the organization had set up an office in December 1942. That office took advantage of its location in neutral Switzerland so that the OSE could communicate with the rest of the world and also maintain contact with headquarters in Chambéry, which greatly helped the organization realize its undercover activities.

Thanks to those lists, we now have the information we need—as in your case, where you're trying to track down those two children.

Madame Pasteur paused.

After extensive, detailed preparations, the plan was activated in March 1943. Groups of six to ten children began to be formed, to be led by guides under direct order from the OSE who would follow precise instructions to reach and cross the Swiss border.

Thus several groups of children eluded the fate that awaited them. But with the Italian capitulation in 1943, the Nazis stationed guards at the Franco-Swiss border, obliging the OSE to suspend its activities for three months. When they began again, under the direction of George Loinger, they decided to change the escape route and followed the course of the Avre River from the town of Annemase to a forest near the Swiss border. They rested there and then—with help from Annemase municipal officials and other collaborators who had studied the German sentries' movements—were able to cross into Switzerland. Employing these tactics and upping the number of children from twelve to twenty-five, they managed to liberate more than a thousand children as well as a large number of adults.

Nevertheless, on February 8, 1944, the Gestapo carried out a raid on OSE headquarters in Chambéry, placing seven directors as well as a number of visitors who happened to be there at the time under arrest. It brought all the organization's activities to an end.

"But what happened to Ariel and Ethel?" Evelyn asked in anguish.

"They were part of Klaus Barbie's Gestapo roundup," Madame Pasteur answered.

At nine o'clock in the morning on that fateful day in 1944, three vehicles pulled up to Maison Izieu: Klaus Barbie's car and two truckloads of German soldiers who burst into the house and brandished their rifles as they tossed the terrified, sobbing children into the rear of the trucks like sacks of potatoes.

They immediately arrested all the teachers except Leon Leifman and Sabine Zlatin.

They were jailed in Montluc Fort, in Lyon, where they were interrogated until nightfall. The following day, some of the captured adults and the older children were moved to Drancy aboard passenger trains.

Thirty-four children, accompanied by Lea Feldblum and two other adults, were deported to Auschwitz and—other than Lea—were sent to the gas chambers. She was the only survivor who could attest to what happened.

"Oh my God, what a terrible end happened to my poor children," Evelyn said as she wept. "After such an intense search I thought I would find them alive, or at least that I might meet some of their descendants... They don't know how much their fate has hurt me," she said as she put her head into her hands and began to cry inconsolably.

"My dear girl, all of that is over now," said Madame Pasteur, embracing her. "If nothing else, you leave here knowing that no one can hurt them anymore."

"At least that's true," Evelyn muttered with resignation.

Chapter 21

Evelyn reached her hotel room. Closing the door softly in case her grandmother was still sleeping, she moved forward slowly to avoid making noise and felt all but overwhelmed by exhaustion.

"Evelyn, is that you?"

"Yes, Grandma, it's me," she responded as she opened the door to the bedroom where her grandmother was.

"How did your research go?" she asked with curiosity.

Evelyn approached her and gave her a kiss, then sat down next to her and took her grandmother's hand. "I'd say well, since I met a woman named Margot Pasteur. She worked at Maison Izieu and knows almost every detail of what happened back then, thanks to an organization called the OSE. It had the foresight to compile complete lists of all the children and instructors that lived in the houses they created, and to protect thousands of kids from assured deportation—at least until the Nazis disbanded them."

"So what happened to them?" Lea asked with keen interest.

"It's a long, very sad story," Evelyn replied anxiously. "I'm sorry you didn't feel well this morning, when we decided to see what we could find out there. I feel like I learned a lot about what happened before and after the war."

"I would have liked to have gone with you so much," Lea said with a sigh. "But lately I've been so depressed and it's giving me terrible headaches."

"Grandma, I swear I'm going to help you find out what happened to your sons, no matter what it costs. There's nothing more I can do about Duvid, Bluma, Ariel and Ethel; they were all sent to Auschwitz on freight trains and ended up dead in the crematorium," she added as she cried.

"My God," Lea exclaimed in horror. "They were in the very prime of their lives."

"You're right, Grandma. In his madness and lust for power, Hitler carried out an unnamed genocide against the Jews he hated, supported by a nation in social and economic disarray that blindly obeyed without understanding that its actions were a malign impulse—and who didn't foresee the consequences."

When she saw her grandmother blanch, she decided to change the subject. "I spoke to Jonathan on the phone yesterday and he said that, thank God, everyone in the family is fine; he says hello. We were talking about the miracle that has happened—that I'm no longer suffering from those nightmares nor any horrifying daydreams. Because we've been so busy with our investigation, I hadn't realized I was resting nights without interruption. I thought it was just because every day's activities had tired me out."

"My beautiful Evelyn," Lea said, "you don't know how happy I am that we made this trip, since you've accomplished to overcome the torment of those nightmares and can get on with your life."

"It's true, Grandma. I feel like I'm free from the ghosts of the past, phantoms that tormented me unrelentingly. I'm so thankful Dr. Eidelman suggested this trip, so grateful to my parents for supporting me the whole time, to Jonathan for trusting me and to you for being there on every step of this long, long journey."

"You can count on me always."

"I love you so much, Grandma," Evelyn answered as they embraced, "and I promise from this moment on I'm going to dedicate every moment I have to helping you find your children."

Chapter 22

"Grandma, where are you?" Evelyn called out as she searched the hotel room.

"I'm on the terrace," Lea answered right away, unaccustomed to hearing her granddaughter speak so loudly.

"Grandma, I have some very good news," she announced as she embraced Lea excitedly.

"What's this all about,?"

"It's about your boys Joel and Michael!"

"But what are you saying?" Lea answered nervously.

"Grandma, sit down, because you look really nervous to me," Evelyn said in an attempt to calm her down. Once Lea was seated on the sofa, Evelyn began to relate what had happened.

This morning I got up very early and when I saw you were still asleep I decided to go downstairs and have just a little something for breakfast. Once I finished eating, I didn't have anything to do while I was waiting for you to wake up so I decided to go to the hotel business center. I got on a computer and opened Facebook to see what was new with my friends and other people I know, and then it occurred to me to look into whom else I might find, so I did a search on Joel Wolovisky. To my surprise the name showed up and when I dug a little deeper I discovered he's a doctor in Israel. So then I did a search for his specialty and for a number where I could reach him.

Once I got the number and found out he was a cardiologist, I called the medical office and asked for Dr. Joel Wolovisky. I explained to the receptionist that I was a relative of the doctor's, from the United States, and that I wanted to confirm if he was the person we had been looking for.

"How may I be of assistance, Miss?"

"I want to know if the doctor's father is named Elias and if he has a brother named Michael."

"That's correct, Miss. The doctor's father is dead but his brother lives in Tel Aviv, just as he does."

"Thank you so much for this information," I told her as I was feeling a rush of adrenaline. Suddenly my heart was pounding.

"Oh my God, it can't be true," Lea exclaimed excitedly.

"But it is, Grandma—it's them. There's no doubt in my mind." Lea began to cry uncontrollably.

"But, Grandma, what's wrong, why are you crying?" Evelyn asked, concerned.

"I'm crying from the overwhelming emotion I'm feeling, imagining that soon I'll be with my sons."

"That's what I was thinking, Grandma. Instead of returning to the States, why don't we go on to Israel? We're halfway there already."

"God bless you, Evelyn, for what you've just told me—and for all your help."

"So let's move forward with our idea. Call Grandpa Abraham, tell him what has happened and ask him what he thinks about the trip to Israel."

"I'll call him right away," she answered excitedly.

Soon Lea came back to her granddaughter to tell her that her husband was not only in favor of the trip to Israel, but that he had advised her to use any resource necessary to find her sons.

"That's great, Grandma. Now I need to call Mom, Dad and Jonathan to tell them about our plans." Lea nodded and Evelyn gave her grandmother a kiss on the cheek before going into her room to talk on the phone privately.

"Hey, baby," Evelyn heard Jonathan say on the other end of the line. "I love you so much and you don't know how much I miss you. But at least there are only a few days before you come back. I can't hold out any longer."

"Jonathan," Evelyn said, pausing before going on. "I love you, too, very much—and I miss you even more—but something has come up. Something we have got to resolve, so we can't come home right away."

"What are you talking about?" he asked, confused. "I thought you were coming back to the States in three days. That's what you told me the last time we talked."

"I know I did. But it turns out I didn't know that during

the time my grandmother lived in Poland, she was married and had two sons. When she immigrated to the US, she couldn't bring them with her. She had been trying to track them down in Poland, on this trip, but she couldn't. She got so depressed she wasn't eating, she didn't want to go out with me and she slept all day long. I'd begun to think she was sick. But this morning I awoke with the idea of how I might be able to find her sons and it turned out to be easier than I thought. They are in Israel. And everyone from Grandpa Abraham to my parents—I just hung up with them—agrees we should go to Israel."

"What an unbelievable story!" Jonathan said, unable to contain himself.

"You don't know how surprised I was when I got all this straight from my grandmother's mouth," Evelyn quickly responded. "I always saw her as this very beloved, very reserved figure, always a lady, and yet sometimes I felt she was withdrawn, absent. I thought it was part of her, how she is, but now I know how terrible it's been to live with such a traumatic experience. Now I understand the ups and downs of her personality."

"Evelyn, sweetheart," Jonathan answered tenderly, "I understand what you're going through and even though I'm going crazy to see you, I, too, am asking you to do everything possible to help your grandmother find her children. I'll be here, waiting for you, with open arms."

Chapter 23

The El-Al jet touched down at Ben Gurion Airport in Israel.

Evelyn peered from her window, ecstatic, following all the maneuvers airport staff made, also thinking of how fortunate it felt to return to the Promised Land. When she turned to share a thought with Lea, she noted the deep emotion that had taken hold of her. She even feared something might happen given her advanced age.

"Grandma, please, stay calm; there's so much we have to do. I don't want your blood pressure to go up and then have to find a doctor."

"I'll try to calm down," Lea answered quickly. "But the fact is, it's like there's a volcano that's about to erupt inside of me. I'm experiencing a mix of memories, sorrow, dread, happiness, love and fear."

"What are you scared of, grandma?"

"Afraid that my children will reject me for having

abandoned them," she answered with anguish.

"I don't think that will happen after all these years," Evelyn reassured her.

"God willing, so it will be," Lea all but implored as she raised her hand to her heart.

After that brief conversation, there was no more time to exchange ideas. They needed to devote their full attention towards getting through the airport, passport control and baggage claim. They boarded a taxi and gave him instructions to go to the Sheraton Tel Aviv hotel. At that moment, they were able to plan again how they would meet up with Joel Wolovisky.

"Evelyn," said Lea, looking into her eyes, "I want to drop the bags at the hotel and go on to my son's practice right away."

"Grandma, don't you think we should get to the hotel, rest a while, and then after we have lunch we can go to the practice? I'm sure we're going to have to wait until the doctor has seen all the patients who have an appointment before they are going to let us in."

"You're completely right, Evelyn. I'm letting my heart run away with me while you are thinking with your head."

"Here we are, Grandma," Evelyn remarked as she watched the taxi maneuver around a traffic circle and then stop in front of the hotel.

As soon as they got upstairs to their room and handed over a tip to the bellman, Evelyn suggested Lea lie down for a while to recover the energy she would need that afternoon.

"Thank you for suggesting that," Lea told her as she

made her way to the bedroom; she felt very tired. Evelyn followed her with her eyes until she left her sight, and then went about unpacking.

Once she had finished her task, she went out to the terrace and sat down on a metal chair that was next to a round table with three other seats. She took in the balcony's breathtaking view that included the ocean, the beach and all the people headed there to enjoy its natural wonders. She couldn't stop thinking about the contrast that awaited them later, when Lea would tell her son that she was his mother.

"Please, God," she asked aloud from the very depths of her heart. "Don't let Joel Wolovisky reject my Grandma—it would mean the end of her days if he did."

At three in the afternoon, Lea and Evelyn stepped out of the taxi and walked over to the clinic where a sign read in Hebrew:

JOEL WOLOVISKY
CARDIOLOGIST

"Good afternoon, Madam," Evelyn greeted the receptionist in English.

"How may I help you, Miss?" the receptionist answered warmly.

"My grandmother and I are members of Dr. Wolovisky's family and we would like to request a few minutes of his time, to talk."

"As you can see, the doctor has appointments with a

number of patients but if you wish to wait until he is done, I can ask him if he has time to see you following his appointments."

Evelyn agreed with a nod and they went to sit down in the waiting room as they saw the receptionist get up from her desk and head toward the doctor's examination room.

"The doctor will see you when he finishes his appointments," the receptionist confirmed as soon as she returned to the waiting room, increasing the anxiety that Lea felt.

"Thank you for your help," Evelyn told her. "We will wait for as long as it takes."

Three hours passed and as Lea began to suffer from such a long delay, she heard that they were being called: "Please come this way—the doctor is waiting to see you."

"Come in," Dr. Wolovisky said to them, rising from his desk. "Have a seat." He pointed to two chairs that had been placed just in front of his desk. "So, how can I help you?" he asked the women, curiously.

Lea observed him for some time, admiring his shiny, dark brown hair, his lofty bearing, slim and resolute...and at that very moment she experienced a heavy pounding in her heart. There was no doubt the man was her son.

"My name is Lea Rotlewicz," she said with emotion. "In 1929 I lived in Poland and I was married to Elias Wolovisky..." She hesitated, but then went on. "There were two children, Joel and Michael, from that marriage."

Dr. Wolovisky took a deep breath, then asked excitedly: “Are you my mother?”

“Yes, son, I am your mother, who has finally found her children after so many years of intense searching.”

“Thank you God,” he added, almost out of breath. “Mom, Michael and I have looked everywhere for you,” he said as he got out of his seat and hurried over to take her in his arms.

Evelyn looked on as the two strongly embraced and tears fell from their eyes, the result of the overwhelming emotions both felt at that moment.

“My son—my beloved son—how I have longed for this moment,” she said as they embraced.

“And how I have looked for you, too! I thought I saw the mother I could never forget in every woman who crossed my path—the mother who had shown such love for us, who sang songs and taught us so much, who was so important in our lives, yet who disappeared so suddenly and completely, without any explanation. Mom, let me call Michael so he can come meet you,” Joel said, letting go of her arm. “I want to share the happiness that is washing over us right now.”

As soon as the conversation with his brother ended, he hung up and exclaimed that Michael was headed over immediately.

“Joel,” Lea said excitedly, “I want you to meet Evelyn. She’s my granddaughter and your niece.” Joel threw out his arms and as she hurried over to him, they embraced.

“What a beautiful niece I have!”

“And I have a cardiologist uncle who’s famous

throughout Israel."

"Oh, that's not such a big deal..." he answered, overjoyed. It was then they heard the door open. A man that looked remarkably like Joel came in.

"Michael, I want you to meet our mother," Joel said as he gestured to Lea.

"Oh, Mom, I've missed you so much!" he exclaimed and then hugged her. Joel joined them and the three embraced, strongly, as they savored such an incredible moment.

After a while, Joel suggested they go into the waiting room and have a coffee, to share respective stories that needed to be told. Once they were seated, Lea spoke first.

"This is the most emotional moment I have ever lived," she declared as she looked at her sons.

For years I asked myself what would happen if we met again and in my dreams I saw a reunion like the one we are living right now. But when I'd awaken I suffered terrible disappointment and intense sadness.

I want to explain why I left, but I ask you to understand that the circumstances that drove me to do it were stronger than I was.

I met Elias at a gathering when I was fifteen, at my parents' house. That was where they told me that in just a few months he was to be my husband.

I felt I was way too young to take on the responsibilities of marriage for which I was not prepared. In private I dreamt that some other young man with whom I could fall in love would come along.

I asked my parents not to make me marry Elias, who was so much older than I, but they refused to listen and declared there was a promise between the two families—that they could not break their word, which they had already given.

I cried, I begged, but it was all in vain. A few months later we were married and we went to live in a small house that Elias owned.

At the beginning of our time together, Elias treated me with a certain deference, but after a few days he began to drink, and most of the time he did so to such excess that he began to lose control. It left me desolate and fearful. I ran to my parents' house to complain and ask them to do something, but they refused to believe me despite the fact that I had always behaved exactly as they expected when I lived with them.

Time passed slowly and my desperation grew more acute, especially when he began to shout at me and treat me harshly, at will.

"Please! Help me!" I begged my parents. But they had nothing to offer except endless admonitions about how I was supposed to behave to improve my marriage.

One fateful night after we had relations, he shouted at me and kicked me so severely that I decided to kill myself. I didn't think there was any other way to end such misery.

But an important event kept me from going through with it. I discovered I was pregnant. You were born, Joel, and it filled me with such happiness that I put my own life on a secondary plane and dedicated myself completely to your care. Then I found out I was pregnant for a second time and I had a beautiful boy whom we decided to call Michael, in memory of Elias's father who had just died.

Elias was quite pleased by your births and he made time to see you and play with you every day. It moved me to see you all, but as soon as he went back to drinking he would become impossibly irritable with me. I always wondered how a person with such extreme behaviors could actually exist.

One day I met Abraham Rotlewicz, at a time when Elias's abuse had grown so extreme that I had to look for help and I found it in the man who is my husband today. But I could never be completely happy because despite the fact that Abraham is a good man and that we have lived comfortably and had a child together; there was not a moment in my life when I didn't think of you.

"Why didn't you take us with you, Mom?" Michael asked, intrigued.

"Elias would have searched for us to the ends of the earth and he would have killed me, leaving you both without a mother and with a father in prison. My only consolation was always thinking that Elias's conduct, where you were concerned, was caring, despite his drinking. In addition I was certain that Vera, his mother—was going to look out for you."

"Oh, Mom!" Joel exclaimed, overwhelmed. "I'm so sorry your relationship was so toxic and that you had to suffer in that way. By listening to what you have to say, I've been able to understand why you left. But you left behind such a void in our lives that I think we will never manage to understand it all."

"I'm so, so sorry," Lea responded, sick at heart. "I just want to confess to you that I made a mistake—I don't know if it was because I was so young and inexperienced, or came from the desperation that being around Elias, and the way he was, created in me. But I want to tell you that if I had it to do all over again, I wouldn't hesitate to fight to keep you beside me, regardless of the cost."

"Thank you, Mom," Michael said, drawing near to protect her within his arms. "I needed to hear those words of love, as a way to close out a chapter in my life that left me unable to feel like anyone else who had been raised with the affection and support of a mother."

Michael went back to his seat, and Joel took the opportunity to speak.

One day we went to visit our grandparents and when we came home you weren't there, which stuck us as very strange. We looked for you everywhere, but to no avail. That night when father got in and we asked about you, he didn't know how to respond. It led us to feel this terrible uncertainty as well as intense pain.

The following day, Dad went to Grandma Vera so she would take care of us and from that moment on he never spoke of you again, as if you were dead. He became a taciturn, withdrawn man. With all that, he never remarried nor did we ever know any woman in whom he might have been interested. We always thought that maybe he lived on memories of you and that he never got over your leaving.

When the socio-economic situation in Poland began to worsen, my father—who struggled to make a living and who hoped to distance himself from orthodox religion—decided we should move to Vienna, which had previously been part of the Austro-Hungarian Empire.

It was a terrible burden to be separated from our grandparents, whom we had loved so, especially Grandma Vera, who always looked after us so devotedly.

Vienna was a cosmopolitan and very beautiful city where great stock was placed in culture, art and music. Papa found a Viennese lady named Erika who looked after us while he dedicated himself to his textile business.

"Forgive me for interrupting you, Joel," Michael said emotionally. "But I wanted to tell them a little about what I remember about Vienna." Joel nodded in agreement and his brother went on.

We lived on Franz Hochedlinzer Street and attended a public school, called Pazmanitengasse that was near our house, but what I remember most affectionately was when Frau Erika would take us on trips to the Vienna Woods and the Danube.

One day that I'll never forget, we were coming back after an excursion on the Danube when some Viennese children who hated Jews began to throw stones at us and shouted at us to leave and never return. Back then we didn't understand the reason for the attack since we hadn't started it.

When we reached our house and we told Papa what had happened, we realized that something strange was happening. He didn't want to tell us anything else... He thought we were too small to understand the magnitude of the problem. Now we know that in 1932, Austrian Chancellor Engelbert Dolfuss, who represented the Christian Socialist party, took power. He was a fascist and a great admirer of Mussolini's, who imposed an anti-democratic constitution. However, Hitler and the Austrian Nazis opposed Chancellor Dolfuss's mandate because they sought Germany's political and economic annexation of the nation.

When Hitler assumed power in 1933, most Austrians' desire to stand by the Nazis intensified.

Dolfuss decided to dissolve the parliament, abolish the Nazi party and govern by decree, but the Nazis began to stage disturbances; terrorism increased. Dolfuss was taken prisoner and then killed.

On March 12, 1938 Hitler's troops entered Austria and German annexation became a reality.

As soon as a National-Socialist government was set up in Austria, efforts were begun to expel Jews from every sphere of national life, to confiscate their factories and businesses, to suppress freedom of expression, freedom of the press and seize Jews' residences, synagogues and schools as well as imprison or murder their leaders.

The Austrian invasion marked the beginning of the extermination of two hundred thousand Austrian Jews and more than one hundred thousand non-Aryan Christians.

The moral and material conditions affecting Austria's Jews became insufferable and as acts of barbarism intensified, my father, concerned for our lives, decided we should go to Palestine.

"The urgency to leave Vienna took my brother and me by surprise," added Joel.

We were just a couple of kids who didn't understand how dire the moment was and the luck we'd had to get out in time. The idea of leaving behind daily routines, friends and Frau Erika—our greatest support—was intolerable to us.

Our arrival in Palestine was quite difficult since in addition to not knowing the language, we didn't have any suitable place to live, but before leaving Vienna, Papa had managed to get in touch with a childhood friend named Isaac Mendel. He met us at our boat and offered to put us up in his house until we found a decent place to set up our permanent residence.

Isaac's wife was named Milka and they had two daughters our age named Talia and Esther, who welcomed us warmly. That was so important to us for feeling better about the twists life had sent our way.

A month and a half passed before we could find a house to rent, but we were truly content to have some privacy and a bigger space for what we needed.

Papa explained to us that at the end of the nineteenth century, Zionist immigration to Palestine and a renaissance of the Hebrew language had begun under British auspices during the First World War, at the time of the 1917 Balfour Declaration. The English invaded the city of Jerusalem and a month later, in 1922, Palestine fell within the British mandate. Non-Jewish Palestinians initiated anti-British uprisings in 1920, 1929 and 1936, but to no end.

In 1947, with the end of the Second World War and the Holocaust, the British government terminated its mandate in Palestine and the United Nations General Assembly voted to partition the region into separate Jewish and Arab states. The Jews accepted the proposition but the Arabs were opposed, which led them to initiate a civil war as the State of Israel was formed in 1948.

Starting then our lives began to improve since beneath the British mandate we had felt subjugated. But with the formation of the State of Israel, we felt that for the first time the land was ours and that any efforts we made on its behalf would be worth the trouble.

Chapter 24

Lea pressed the doorbell outside her son Joel's house then heard some rapid footsteps draw near. A little boy answered the door.

"Are you my grandmother?" asked Asher, watching her with an innocent expression.

"Yes, my darling boy, I'm your grandma," Lea answered as she knelt to be at eye level with the boy. "How old are you?"

"I'm ten," Asher answered. Taking advantage of the moment, he hugged her tightly and excitedly. "My grandmother Raquel—my mother's mother—died a long time ago, and after that my grandfather Elias, and I felt very sad because now there weren't going to be any other grandparents to laugh or play with. But today my dad said that you came looking for us and I feel like I'm the happiest boy in the world. He also told me I'm going to meet another grandpa named Abraham who lives in the United States."

Evelyn had come over to them after parking the car in front of the house and she watched as Lea's eyes filled with tears from the emotion she was feeling. She continued to hug the child with deep tenderness.

"And who are you?" asked Asher, abandoning his grandmother's arms when he saw another woman come up.

"I'm your cousin Evelyn."

"Papa, Mama," the boy shouted out, "I don't just have a new grandmother; I've got a grown-up cousin." Lea and Evelyn exchanged looks of true joy.

"Come in, please," a young woman requested in English that bore traces of an Israeli accent. "My name is Ruth," she added right away. "Joel's wife."

"It's a pleasure, Ruth," Lea said, excited to discover who such an attractive woman was.

"The pleasure is all mine," Ruth replied, holding out her hand in greeting. Lea, however, went over to her and embraced her affectionately, remembering words Joel had said regarding the fidelity and devotion that his wife had demonstrated since their marriage.

"Ruth, I want to introduce you to Evelyn, my granddaughter—and your cousin," she added.

"I'm delighted to know you," Ruth replied at once.

"No, the pleasure is mine," Evelyn hastened to say.

"Come this way," Ruth asked. "The others are dying to see you." In response to their hostess's invitation, they stepped into the vestibule, decorated in simple, contemporary furnishings, and as they moved toward the living room they caught sight of a pleasant environment where that style was extended with light wooden furniture upholstered and accessorized in earth tones.

"Mom, Evelyn, what a joy it is that you're here," Joel exclaimed when he saw they'd come, and taking their hands excitedly, he said: "Well, you've already met my wife, Ruth, and Asher; and this is my youngest, Benjamin, who's six." Lea went over to the boy, took him into her arms and kissed him. The boy, remembering something his father had told him, let himself be embraced without fear.

"Mom..." Michael spoke. He went over to her and put his arm around her shoulders, guiding her to where his wife and son were. "...I want you to meet Jenny and our baby, Samuel." Lea embraced them silently as Jenny offered an emotional welcome.

"Madam Lea, it's a real pleasure to meet you. Please have a seat with us—you, too, Evelyn," she added with enthusiasm. "Michael has told me so much about you."

"It's the same with me," Evelyn answered. "I so wanted to meet you all. You are family and as an only child it makes me happy to have aunts, uncles and cousins." The evening went on amid anecdotes, memories of the past and other emotions within a welcoming and relaxed atmosphere.

Ruth and Jenny had prepared a traditional Israeli meal with salads and marvelous desserts, served atop a table covered in imported white linen and multi-colored flowers; they had brought out their finest china as well, used only on the most special occasions.

They played music, sang, danced, and played with

the children until they were exhausted. "Let's put the kids to bed," said Ruth when she saw Benjamin asleep on an armchair.

"I'll carry him," Joel said, going over to the boy and picking him up easily.

"I'll go with you," added Jenny, carrying an also slumbering Samuel in her arms.

"May I come with you?" Evelyn pleaded.

"Yes, of course, come with us," Ruth answered. I can use another hand. When it comes time to put the boys down, we need all the help we can get."

Asher went over to Lea, kissed her and asked, all but begging: "Please don't forget us, grandma."

"Oh, no, darling," she responded as she embraced him. "I'll be expecting you soon at my house and I promise that Grandpa Abraham and I will take you to Disney World."

"Whoa!" the boy shouted with joy. "I knew it was going to be great to have a grandmother again."

"Ok, say goodnight," Ruth exhorted.

"Good night, grandmother. I love you very much."

"Good night, Asher, and May God bless you." The boy glanced at her one more time and then holding out his hand to his mother, went off to his bedroom.

"Mom, I want to talk to you," Michael asked, inviting her to sit beside him on the living room sofa. "I was waiting for the right moment to speak to you alone," he added with a serious expression.

"What is it, son? Tell me," Lea answered, anxious to hear what he might say.

"Mom, I don't want to take away from the happiness you're feeling right now after finding your adult sons, each with his own family, in an apparently idyllic set-up, especially since I know that tomorrow you return to the USA and this will all seem like a dream. I want to share some things with you that have kept me from being happy. Maybe if I get them off my mind I can reach that peace that always eludes me." Lea nodded and encouraged him to go on.

"When you left," he added, in a devastated tone, "my world just fell apart."

"Where is my mother?" I wondered every day and I asked the same thing of my grandmother, Vera, time and again when I'd see her. "All the kids have a mother except Joel and me," I'd repeat to her, and she'd look at me sadly, not knowing what to say, or do, but now I understand that she, too, was wondering what had happened to make you run off that way.

Lea sought to speak, but Michael went on, ignoring her.

At first our friends looked on us with pity, thinking that something bad had happened to you, but as time went on and they saw you didn't come back, there began to be rumors from ill-natured people who began to speculate why you were absent and they thought it might be the case you'd walked out on us to run off with a lover. They started to make fun of Joel and me.

One day I worked up the courage and I asked Joel what he thought of those rumors. He answered, "Don't pay any attention to those people. They don't have any-

thing better to do and they make stuff up. You and I will look for mom, wherever she may be, and we're going to show the world that there was no way she could have abandoned us."

That was when I decided to join forces with Joel to take on the most important search of our lives. We began by asking Dad about you and he answered he had no interest in your whereabouts and asked us never again to mention your name as long as he lived.

Everywhere we went, we kept on asking everyone who knew you, but no one knew anything that could shed any light on our disquiet. One day Papa told us we were going to emigrate to Vienna, and that, for us, was the beginning of the end. How were we going to find you—how would you ever find us—if we were going to another country?

We begged Papa not to move—that he leave us behind with our grandparents—but he wouldn't budge and reminded us they wanted to stay in Poland—he hadn't been able to convince them to emigrate with us. "Then let's all stay here," we asked him several times. But his mind was made up and there was no argument strong enough to dissuade him.

We left Poland with our hearts in tatters, and unable to hold back, we asked Papa once more when we'd see you again. He didn't answer. So we cried and cried thinking that we'd never see you again, coupled with the fact that we were leaving our grandparents behind, especially Grandma Vera, as well as friends and all the other people that made up our world.

Time passed and Joel got used to things. As for me, I could see how hard it was to trust people, and it got to the point where I began to withdraw from everyone around me, even my friends, and became a real loner. When I was a teenager, I didn't want anything to do with girls my age until one day I met Nora. I thought I could tell her my problems and we got married. But it didn't last very long. I realize now it was my fault; it was really hard for me to trust her and I began to keep tabs on everything she did.

We fought the same fights all the time until she just couldn't cope anymore and she told me that although she loved me, she had to leave because our relationship was turning into madness. I let her go with a profound wound in my heart because I knew that although I loved her, I was also doing her irreparable harm.

That was when I decided to seek out psychiatric help. After I told my story to the doctor, he explained to me that the root of my problem originated in the hurt that your abandonment and silence had caused us. I have to confess to you that at that point I hated you to the depths of my soul. I hated you for your indifference and estrangement and for your lack of maternal instincts. How could you walk out on us that way?

"I'm so sorry, son—so sorry," she said in a flood of tears. "I didn't want to do anything to harm you but neither could I resign myself to my fate beside an angry alcoholic. I was too young to understand the future consequences of my acts. Please, son, forgive me," she begged him desperately.

"What's going on in here?" Joel asked as he came into the living room.

"I was telling Mom about the problems I've had in life," Michael said, worn out.

"Enough with all that!" Joel replied. "Times like these should be happy! It's nothing short of an authentic miracle that we have been able to find each other after so many years. We should give thanks to God that it has happened and try to be a family that stays together through love. The past doesn't matter—it doesn't exist. Let's look at the present with optimism and try to enjoy every moment life offers us."

"Mom, I'm so sorry," Michael excused himself regretfully. "Joel's right. The past is the past and I promise you won't get any more reproaches from me."

"I also regret so much what you had to go through in my absence," Lea declared with resolve. "And I want to say again that if God were to grant me another chance I would never repeat the error of abandoning you. Please—please—forgive me!"

"We've already forgiven, you, Mom," Joel replied compassionately. "And I'll be thankful if you never ask for forgiveness again."

"Thank you, son," Lea said, in an all but inaudible tone.

"I love you so much, Mom," Joel reassured her.

"I do, too," said Michael as he came over to hug her.

"What's up here? Did I miss something important?" Evelyn inquired.

"We were just remembering the past," said Joel with

finality. “Everything’s settled and forgotten.”

“Grandma, you look tired to me,” said Evelyn, observing her swollen eyes and sad countenance. “I think it’s time we headed back to the hotel. I want you to get a good night’s rest since tomorrow we've got to travel.” Lea nodded and stood.

Ruth and Jenny came into the room and farewells ensued. Every member of the family approached Lea and Evelyn to wish them a bon voyage, give them a hug, and repeat how much they looked forward to a reunion in the United States, two months hence, when the children would be out of school on their summer vacations.

Chapter 25

Lea settled into her airplane seat beside Evelyn, fastened her seatbelt and felt her heart race as a consequence of the conflicting emotions she felt in those moments.

On one hand there had been the search for her children, finding them and the excitement of sharing her presence with them and their beautiful families in the State of Israel with all its splendor and magnificence, and finally saying goodbye. Yet on the other hand, there was the newfound distance—though with the promise of a reunion in the near future.

"Grandma, are you okay?" Evelyn asked, nervous, as she saw the tension in the older woman's face.

"Yes, darling. I was just thinking of everything that has happened on this trip and above all saying goodbye to my sons, who stayed with us all the way to the last moments at the airport—something we didn't expect."

"They are really good people," Evelyn added, convinced of such. “It's very easy to like them. Finding their mother has been a really important element in their lives.”

“Thank you, God, for allowing me to see them and be with them, even if it was late in life,” Lea exclaimed.

“Grandma, they promised to come to Florida in the summer, which is just two months away,” Evelyn said in an effort to soothe her. “So now I want you to take your blood pressure medicine and rest since we’ve got a long flight ahead of us and getting in is going to be very emotional since we’ll be seeing the people we love after so much time.” Lea took the medicine then looked out the window and noted how late it was. She settled into her reclined seat and closed her eyes.

The flight was exemplary and the morning shone in its very best colors. Getting off the plane in Miami was without incident.

“There they are!” Victor shouted, spotting them as soon as they cleared customs.

“Dad, Mom,” Evelyn called out to them, moved. Victor and Vivian ran over to embrace them.

“How I’ve missed my beautiful girls!” he exclaimed, unable to contain himself.

“How we missed you, too,” Evelyn answered immediately.

“Jonathan had to go on an very important business trip for two days,” Vivian said suddenly. “He told me to tell you he was so sorry not to have been here to welcome you.”

“That’s all right, Mom. I’d have liked to have seen

him just now, but what can you do?" Evelyn said with resignation.

"Let me get these suitcases," Victor suggested. "Dad is waiting for us in the car. He's very anxious to see you—and we want to hear more details of the trip."

The following morning, Evelyn went to Dr. Eidelman's office thanks to intervention on the part of her father, who had managed to get her an appointment.

"Good morning, Evelyn," the doctor said courteously, pulling out a chair that was in front of his desk so she could have a seat.

"Thanks for seeing me so soon," Evelyn said as she settled into the chair. "I needed to speak to you to thank you for your dedication and advice. I feel like a different woman ever since the nightmares and visions stopped repeating themselves, and it happened as I emerged from the crossroads where I was—something that seemed impossible. I never thought that problems from the past could have an effect on present-day life. But now I understand that a person's concern and love for others can survive over time—and over the course of several lives."

"That's true, Evelyn," the physician reassured her with conviction. "I've been able to prove that reincarnation exists in your case and in the case of several patients whom I have had to hypnotize and carry over to the time that their phobias began. I've been amazed listening as their minds traveled to previous lives that were different than those they were living in the present, alongside the range of languages, countries and circumstances they had to face. It makes me think the soul does exist and that it bears the mark of every lived experience."

"I am in complete agreement, doctor," Evelyn added. "The circumstances that led me to try to discover the mystery of my past life were too much to ignore. I had the benefit of your professional guidance to solve the problems that afflicted me daily and that prevented me from living like a normal person. Now I can move forward with my life. Thank you for your support. I admire you as a doctor and for being such a sensitive human being, capable of perceiving the aid your patients need," Evelyn declared as she got up to leave.

"I greatly appreciate your words, Evelyn. I'll never forget them—or for you letting me participate in a case as interesting as yours," Dr. Eidelman reassured her as he extended his hand in farewell.

Evelyn opened the doctor's office door and found Jonathan, who'd been waiting for her at the end of the hall.

"I couldn't bear another day away from you," he said, emotionally, drawing near. "That's why I decided to come home ahead of schedule. I love you, darling," he said, embracing her, "and I'm not going to let anyone, or anything ever keep us apart again."

Made in the USA
Columbia, SC
04 September 2018